AVISHAG

by Adam Howard

Copyright © 2022 by Adam Howard
Cover Art: Books Covered by Stuart Bache
Published by House of Howard Publishing

ISBN:
Paperback: 978-1-945130-30-4
Hardcover: 978-1-945130-31-1
Ebook: 978-1-945130-32-8

All rights reserved.

No part of this book may be reproduced, scanned, or distributed in any printed or electronic form without permission. Please do not participate in or encourage piracy of copyrighted materials in violation of the author's rights. Thank you for respecting the hard work of this author.

This is a work of fiction. Names, characters, places, and incidents either are the product of the author's imagination or are used fictitiously, and any resemblance to locales, events, business establishments, or actual persons – living or dead – is entirely coincidental.

Website: adamhowardbooks.com

Table of Contents

Chapter 1: The Hoary Haired King	1
Chapter 2: An Impotent King	3
Chapter 3: Usurper	5
Chapter 4: Annointing the King	7
Chapter 5: Mercy	9
Chapter 6: Twice Fatherless	13
Chapter 7: More Precious than Rubies	17
Chapter 8: Jilted	19
Chapter 9: Wormwood and a Two-Edged Sword	21
Chapter 10: Trust	23
Chapter 11: Torn	27
Chapter 12: Birds of the Air	33
Chapter 13: Ascending to the Throne	37
Chapter 14: Wisdom	43
Chapter 15: Banished	47
Chapter 16: Home	49
Chapter 17: The Traveler	51
Chapter 18: Washing Pools and Fir Bowers	55
Chapter 19: King's Errand	59
Chapter 20: The Proposition	61
Chapter 21: Searching for Love	63

Chapter 22: The Temple and the Grove	65
Chapter 23: Come up from the Desert	69
Chapter 24: Dark	75
Chapter 25: A Wakeful Heart	81
Chapter 26: Shulamite Returned	85
Chapter 27: Laughed to Scorn	89
Chapter 28: In the Court of Women	91
Chapter 29: I Am the Man	95
Chapter 30: A Listener at the Door	99
Chapter 31: Judgment	101
Chapter 32: The Empty Trestle Board	109
Chapter 33: Departure Denied	113
Chapter 34: Regret	117
Chapter 35: Wake not Love	123

Chapter 1:
The Hoary Haired King

The hoary haired king sits upon his throne. Old age bears down upon his shoulders, he a weathered mountain, snow capped and gray, brittle as shale.

David! Are you the man who slew his tens of thousands, and rushed the fields of Hamath? Was it you who feasted and made merry with Jonathan, and laid in bed with the daughters of Saul? Now, who are you? An ancient, crouched and crooked, upheld by women. You who prowled the plains of the Promised Land, devouring Israel's enemies! Ruddy maned and bloody!

What wage has waging war granted you? And righteousness, what respite? Nothing to the love of little Avishag, the Shulemite. She, a dainty black-eyed girl dancing with your daughters, and you, the psalmist of all songstrels, the most majestic of all minstrels.

Avishag! What joy you bring the king! His clapping hands, his singing harp, his eyes are watered with laughter. You are dew in the night, healing the once lush desert.

You are a princess of Salem, the get of Melchizedek, the solemn King of Peace. What better wife for Solomon, David's wisest son? What better queen for Israel, than the loveliest of all Jerusalem?

OH! Avishag! Beloved daughter of our King and God, I beg of you, do not wake love. All you daughters of Israel, hear me. Do not wake love in its time of sleep.

Sleep, sleep now Avishag. Cry no more for the father

called to heaven early. Cry no more, cold and lonely without your brothers or mother… far away, at home on the plains of Sharon. Be warm, warm in the arms of the once mighty lord.

David, who has need of you, will guard you through the night. Be the living ember in his hands, the flame in his bosom, for death blows upon him like a cold wind, and neither coats nor blankets can shield from the icy draft that blows souls to the land from whence no man returns.

Chapter 2:
An Impotent King

Adonijah, son of David to his wife the festive Haggith, sits in mirth with friends. He trusts the men that surround him. His heavy locks of lovely hair safely shroud his shoulders.

Drinking his father's wine, sitting at his side, is his cousin Joab, a slayer of cousins.

And there sits Abiathar, the priest who would be to David's son a staff, but whispers harming secrets, hisses cunning strife. With his godless mouth the priest betrays his king. Through his words he delivers wickedness.

"David is aged, a tabernacle weathered, its stakes loose and its lines slack, no longer fit to house his soul. For so it is said, 'he lies cold at night, and knows not the love of women.'"

Adonjiah stirs with ambition. He yearns for blessings not promised.

"What use is a fallen tent to Israel? Will the Lord not rather have a pillar, erect and strong, that the temple might stand in Jerusalem? Yet, has my father named a king, anointed a son?"

"There is but one who could stand against you, Lord; Solomon, youngest son of beloved Bathsheba."

"How then am I to be king; I, the eldest son of a forgotten womb? Joab, slayer of princes, killer of mighty men, you sit silent, but I sense your purse-lipped mouth conceals violence."

Joab's youth he spent sowing seeds of hatred.

An Impotent King

Treacherously he slew the righteous. With blood-spattered sandals, he walks the world in wickedness.

So he says, like a white-washed sepulcher full of dead men's bones, "Let it be known, that in the days of his youth and strength, I served David. I have shivered in caves and slaughtered men in battles, all for David. Yes, I slew Absalom, his lovely hair entangled in the thorny tree. This I did for David, who loves his enemies and scorns his friends. His mouth flows with wine and honey when I am near, his bounty he always shares, but his heart is a writhing hive of bees, his smile is a snare. I fear my death when I see him, old as he is, so nearly dead himself.

"I choose life and vigor. For you, cousin, I will rally my men to make you king. As for Solomon, he is a ruddy cheeked lad, beardless, no more than a woman's mouth."

Adonijah shudders, cold within his plotting house. "How I fear the treachery of she who speaks with his lips. For by her cunning, she did bed my father and kill her husband. Yet she holds sway in the house of David. Yet she may cut me at the roots, and plant me in the dusty earth."

Chapter 3: Usurper

David, listen! Whirring wheels. The rattle of wood on rock. Whistling pipes and beating drums. The shouting armies will shake you to solid earth, down from your lofty roof.

"What is this noise? The sounds of wedding or of war? My sons haven't sought my counsel, and I command them not. Who is come to topple my house, and rattle my quaking body down to death?"

It is Adonijah, shining black, and Joab, furious at his back. Brave bearded men follow in their fifties and their hundreds. The people shout and the city roars. A joyous clamor assaults the stony walls.

"Avishag, take me from this noisome height. Hold my arms and guide me to my silent throne. Every step's a burden. Sit me down to rest, far from clacking shields and armor's shining scales. My sons will win the wars. My sons will wed the women. I will rest."

* * *

Now comes to his throne, Bathsheba, most loved of beloved David.

"Woman, why do you cry?"

"Your oaths and words are weak, and people line the streets proclaiming Adonijah King. Shouting joy and feasting pleasure overflow, yet my son does not sit the throne. Did you not swear he would be king? Did you not swear your everlasting word to me?"

Now comes Nathan, prophet-seer.

"Is it proclaimed that Adonijah is King, and I have not heard? For so it is said in the streets, 'Adonijah is King, have you not heard?' Yet here you sit upon the throne. And feasts are feeding hundreds, yet Solomon has not been called. Golden oil runs through Adonijah's gleaming beard, and leaves of laureates rustle in his glistening hair."

David wipes his wife's wet tears, and whisks away her worries. He holds her face with tender care and caresses her glassy features with his wrinkled hands.

"Adonijah was to me a sapling, tenderly planted in the hope he would shade my home, and shield from buffeting winds. Now he has grown, raised up a cedar. Yet, infirm in his foundation, his shade is darkness and his every branch quakes to come crashing in upon my house.

"I am weak, and my soul clings to life, suspended as by spiders' silk. Yet my word is powerful as a bellowing bull, my oaths as clear as ringing bells. I will be heard, and Solomon shall this day give voice as King."

Chapter 4:
Annointing the King

How glorious is Solomon, his garish crown set on golden hair. Braided locks kiss his ruddy cheeks, beardless, soft and bare. He is a youth, so young in years. His thoughts are tender, his wisdom yet unborn.

Nathan has anointed you king.

The people await you, as waking eyes await the dawn's resplendent sheen. You are the sun and a new day to those who have slumbered in the darkness of your father's age.

Be wise, though now you are unknowing. Be strong, though now you shiver. Bless Jerusalem with beauty, that you may always be remembered.

* * *

Adonijah, gaudy in his garden gloats, while Joab drinks the blood of grapes. Mirthful maidens and misled men give laud and laughter, singing kingly hymns that are not theirs, but David's. And Adonijah usurps the earth beneath his feet that is not his, but is his brother's.

Adonijah, you should have drank from the fount of wisdom rather than the spout of wine, for on the hills runs a messenger, swift as a hare pursued, and Solomon's men come like hard-toothed hounds behind, with spears and knives to rend your bowels.

Laughing, Adonijah speaks, "Cease! Cease your pleasures you revelers. Cease and hear the words of the messenger.

Speak! Speak, Jonathan. Ever have you been a friend, and ever have you spoken truth between tooth and tongue."

"Even now am I followed, and fear fills my heart for you, my friend, Adonijah. For Solomon is King. So has Nathan and Zadok made it. It is proclaimed, you are a supplanter, and as planters pull up tares, root and stem, men come to tear you from your place. Flee! Find refuge in that Holy House of Peace, for if you stay in the garden now, surely more than the blood of grapes will soak the ground."

Chapter 5:
Mercy

Crowded round the judgement hall stand judging hearts in every chest.

Adonijah, the horns of God's burning altar would not guard you. Like a corral they have cornered you, and Solomon's men have captured you, a sacrifice sorely caught for Israel's peace.

Solomon speaks, "Brother, I am king, but am first your kin. This quarrel between us must come to righteous end. Show yourself a worthy man, serve me and not one hair of your head shall fall to earth."

Head held high, Adonijah will not bow.

He says, "Look," and every head turns. "David is the ancient olive that bears no fruit, Solomon the green stemmed sprout without branch. Bathsheba's snare is hidden in their grove, and I am the bird that is caught. Are the numberless of Israel to be nurtured by the crafty wife who whispers love in dying men's ears? Are the thousands of Jerusalem to be nourished by the tender shoots sucking at the roots of the gnarled tree? You who sit in judgement, hear my words. Where is Solomon's strength to rule? Did not Jacob wrestle with the Lord and prevail until morning? Did not Father David fall the Giant? God chooses he whose strength is in his arms, that the promises of the Lord might be established, but David has chosen he whose strength is but the sighing breath of a woman! The son whose mind is ruled by his mother's muttering."

Adonijah, the people hiss at you. The women spit at you. Oh that you would be silent that you might be counted among the wise. Oh that you had laid your hand upon your mouth, for you have spoken foolishly in lifting yourself up. You have thought evil and vomited your innermost pride. Your mouth has sentenced you to die.

Bathsheba in her earnest anger speaks, "You who mock your father, and scorn the queen-mother, ravens shall pluck your eyes, and eagles shall feast on your flesh."

Solomon stands to pronounce judgement, "All your sins, brother, may I forgive, treason excepted. Should I let you live, you might murder me in my bed. As the living Lord is my God, you, Adonijah, must surely die."

Noble handsome Adonijah, how pitiful he is, bowed low under bruising blows, fists battering his perfect form.

"Out with him!" the people cry. "Out to be stoned."

Little Avishag, look upon Father David. He quakes in the corner, crouched and crying. For one who so loves his sons, how is he so scorned? For all the promises of the Lord, why must his home be divided with war?

Avishag, move now! Move with compassion, even as your bowels are turned with feeling, pity for the forlorn father, whose suffering he is constrained to endure. None should see their sons bloodied, bashed to death.

On winged feet she leaps, and covers Adonijah with her pinions, a gentle dove shielding the deadly falcon.

"Mercy! Mercy!" she cries. "By God, Solomon reigns, and as a prince he has decreed justice, for it is right to punish the wicked! But it is wickedness to strike down a prince for his uprightness. Mercy, my lord! Have mercy on your brother, though his neck be stiff with pride, and his heart be fat with vanity. Mercy Lord, for love's sweet sake!"

David's eye twinkles. His hope shimmers upon the dews of sadness. "Mercy!" he cries out.

Adonijah looks upon his father, whose burning tears melt his tallowed heart. "Yea! Mercy, my brother! Mercy for such a wretched man as I!"

Solomon's hand upheld upholds mercy's cries. "Desist! Desist, you who are roused to passion. Give space for judgement. Give room for quiet wisdom's silence."

The prince deliberates, whether to deliver, or better to detain . . .

"Go to your house my brother. Sin not again, for the merciful hand of God shall not shield you twice from the stones of justice!"

Chapter 6:
Twice Fatherless

Avishag sits between the legs of the aged king.

As David unbraids her plaited head, he says, "So too will your life be unraveled, and with the passing of time, so will the hurt you feel be as the knots of your hair, only to be remembered as a passing pain; for time unravels the strands of every life, and time dims all memories."

The child looks to the ancient's eyes. "Of what do you speak, Father? What pain?"

"I am dying my little dove. My blood runs thick through my veins, and my heart churns it like butter. Soon, it will not beat. Even the swiftest horse's heart must cease when it has run its final race. And the strongest bull cannot drive the plow through eternal fields."

It is right that you should cry, little maiden, for the most beloved of all who ever loved, now loves you. And he cares for you, even as the ancient tree delights in the little birds that nest within its leaves.

* * *

Though he warred through life until his blade clave to his hand, David cannot conquer death. Four years have passed since Solomon was annointed king, and the cold finally freezes the life from the Lion of Judah.

He speaks to his son, the king, Solomon, saying, "Treat sin with justice, reward righteousness with love, and remember God with reverence. I know you are right with God, for he has sworn that the throne shall always be for my sons. Surely, your every desire shall be granted, and the glory of God will rest upon every grove that you have planted.

"Listen Solomon, my son. Hear the words of my mouth, that God's covenants with me shall be secured, for his word rests bitter in my belly and I must speak it, that your reign might be sweet. The sons of Belial surround you, sprung from the earth to strangle you. Like a pruner pruning, cover yourself. Like a farmer with an iron staff, clear the bushes that bear sour fruit and stab you with their thorns. Clear the land of them. Light fires, that they are utterly consumed. You are wise, and know of whom I speak."

Wisdom he speaks to his sons, and love to his children.

Now Bathsheba weeps upon his bosom.

"Woman, do not cry."

"Comfort me with words, my lord, that my tears may cease."

"You have been as the light of the evening to me, when the sun sets and the horizon has no clouds, like the cool air of twilight and the comforting warmth of the harvest night. I go calmly now, as I would to sleep, for you have loved me through the darkness of my life."

"And I," says Bathsheba, "have loved you, as a sweet song and a clear voice."

"If you love me, guard my heart. Care for little Avi. To Solomon she will be like tender grass, springing up after the rain, nourishment to his soul and for his people."

Bathsheba wets the dying king's hands with tears and kisses. "I will, even as you wish it, my lord, my strength."

Blessed are you David, king after God's own heart. Rest. Breathe one last breath and return to God who gave it.

Bathsheba weeps. The men moan. The women keen. The servants in the halls beat their chests and the people in the streets fall upon their faces in the dust. There is a wailing throughout Israel.

Avishag is among the women who anoint the king for death, wrap him with linen, prepare him for the tomb. Priests and prophets anoint a king for his people. Wives and daughters anoint a king for his Lord.

Though David rejoices in the presence of God, his spirit cries out for Avishag.

Avishag kisses her king. Her tears trickle down his cheeks, his body a dead shell, an empty horn without oil.

She has suffered to see a father die before, mourned the lifeless form. With David's death, she is twice fatherless. She wanders through her days as one who is asleep, eyes closed and in dark places.

A river of lamentation flows after David to his tomb. The hero of Israel's songs is gathered to his Father's home.

Chapter 7:
More Precious than Rubies

Avishag, downy in the dawn of womanhood is too early put with Solomon's concubines. By day she coos. By night she softly cries. The women all are wearied with her wallowing.

To Bathsheba they go, saying, "We cannot sleep, for Avi's mourning never rests. She is full of sorrows, too young to bear them, too early flown the nest."

Bathsheba takes her under wing, as a hen gathers its chicks. "Let her sleep with me in the bed of my husband. The little dove longs for its cote. Taken from her coop, she will fly home again."

* * *

In the morning, Avishag wakes the king, latches his sandals, wraps his body in robes. By lamplight she is replaced by women of riper charms. Another washes Solomon's feet, lets free his hair and anoints his head with oils.

She longs for the love of her betrothed, "Oh Solomon, that you were my brother, that you might comfort me at night. For I am full of sadness, and a brother loves at all times, crafted to comfort a sister's sorrows."

Every day she seeks God in prayer. Often she sits at the tabernacle door, awaiting the tender mercies of her lord.

The king's brother sees her there. "Is this the princess of peace, even she who shielded me, the prince of war?"

* * *

Bathsheba watches her ward wax bright but fears Solomon's abandonment. Avi begins again to prance and play but works at day and weeps at night.

Bathsheba, as a counselor, bows before her king. As a mother, she reproves with speech.

"My son, hear me and understand. A good wife is more precious than rubies, worthier than gold. Have pleasure in Avi. She is yet young, and playful as a fawn, but will soon be perfected as a loving doe."

Solomon does not think but speaks. "She is a lovely fawn, but the grace of womanhood is far from her. Her chest is a wall and her legs stalks of grass. How should I take pleasure of bricks and straw? You ask me to love, not as a husband, but as a father would."

"Drink my son, from this cup your father has given you. Drink from the well your father has dug, and her blessings will spring like rivers, and she will grace the land with fruitfulness. She may be a child, not yet knowing wisdom, but she speaks the law of kindness. Admire her disposition, and later be ravished by her breasts."

Solomon laughs at his mother. "Let her breasts first grow, then I shall know the bounty of her soul. Let me go, for the generals of Egypt are in the city."

Chapter 8: Jilted

King Hurim's cunning craftsmen of curious skill chortle words with strangers' tongues, aliens come to build the house of God. Their voices hum through Solomon's hall; Solomon's hall, broader than the breadth of David's palace, higher than the heights of David's home. All the craft is weal, all the craft is hale, but none of these are so great, none are loved so well as the dear Adon-Hiram, for whom all human hearts do swell.

Priests, prophets, kings and princes, gather for a feast.

Solomon speaks, "David's temple was a curtain tent and ours is risen stone. For him, the sword never rested, and enemies encircled him about, but the soles of our feet find rest on our enemies' throats, and none can rise against us! The Lord has removed our adversaries, and Gezer's every stone is toppled under Egypt's weight. Clap your hands and stomp the rushes, our enemies are threshed and our land filled with riches. Let us build a house up to Almighty God! Hurim has said, let my servants be your force, let their hands tool your stones. To which I say, so mote it be, for there are none among us who hew timber and cut stone as can the men of Lebanon."

Cheers roll against the walls like clashing waves. A great feast is laid before the servants of Israel and the many hands of Tyre. They have traveled across the sea and have hunger for fresh fruit and fat flesh.

Solomon, like the sun in the east, sits risen above the

rest. And Avishag sits beside him, that she might be the horizon for all to look to in his early reign. She beams with the pride of morning's light. All of Solomon's court looks upon her gentle features and loves her.

"Avishag," speaks the king, "take this garment, whole and white, as a sign that I align my house with yours. So as this cloth is one, so will we be sewn, sealed seamlessly together."

"Solomon, I take this garment as a sign, that so long as its strands do clothe me, so to you I am bound. As the Lord wills."

"So mote it be!" Shouts the crowd.

LO! There, a woman of foreign feature enters from the darkness, elegant as a dune, red hued, breasts round as the desert downs. Solomon stands to hush the hissing crowd. "Behold, the Pharaoh's favored daughter, my favorite of all women. Her dowry is Gezer, and she is our reward."

She glides across the stony floors, a mist through the midst of the gathered nations. She ousts little Avishag, shadows her in splendor.

"Rejoice," says Solomon. "Revere your future queen."

You foreigners laud the lovely princess. Cymbals clash, and sticks beat drums, but Israel sits silent. Staring, they do not stand, nor do they sound with joy. Adonijah is among the princes, all in awe-full agreement. The priests too purse their lips and utter not a word, for all are struck with wonder.

Avishag is bent, and Bathsheba bows with disappointment.

Chapter 9:
Wormwood and a Two-Edged Sword

Bathsheba goes again, in private, to her son Solomon.

"Why have you fattened your heart with the fodder of pride, and let pleasures plug your ears with wax? Why will you, my son, be ravished with an alien woman, embrace a stranger to your bosom?"

Solomon speaks, saying, "I have set out and accomplished that which the Beloved could not do. All of that which was promised to Abraham is now to Israel delivered. Yet from your demanding I am not redeemed."

"I fear for you now, Solomon. I fear you have grasped at a breath of wind and all you build will be as sand, and in folly you will go astray."

Solomon answers, "Has the Lord not blessed Israel. Has HE not chosen its path? Then how can Israel go astray, with God as its guide?"

Bathsheba clutches at her son. "The Lord's path is strictly established but the ways of a stranger are slippery. Remove yourself from this marriage and knock not again at the doors of Egypt."

"The Promised Land is a country of fruitfulness, and my wife's lips drip with honey. Her mouth is like cream. Whatever I dream, the Lord has not kept from me. From my heart, he has withheld nothing. There is nothing better for a man than to rejoice in his soul for the blessings of God. You vex me, and beg in vain. Leave now."

"A mother will be heard, her son will listen. Though

this woman's mouth is smooth as oil and the bounty of Egypt drips to Israel as from a honeycomb, the end of this will be bitter as wormwood and sharp as a two-edged sword. Her feet go down to death. Her steps point toward Hell. Leave her, lest your honor leaves you, and strangers harvest the wealth of Israel."

Chapter 10:
Trust

Everyday Prince Adonijah awaits Avishag, but never meets her. He is as the ground, and she a cloud never floating down. He watches her, and sees in her the many shapes of his fantasies. Yet she does not heed him, nor know his daring stares.

Adonijah, love the beautiful Avishag from a distance. Go not near to her, for what is the king's may be had by no other than the king. Mercy may soften a man's heart, but is weak in the face of anger. Raise not your brother's ire to rage, but rather leave in the past your longing for what is his.

* * *

Abiathar has bidden Adonijah come to the Tabernacle on the high mount. They sit and eat together.

"Hear me now, Adonijah," speaks Abiathar the priest. "The Lord has not forsaken you, but has provided you with a gift most precious."

"Speak, priest. I will hear you."

"Solomon has scorned the Lord's chosen queen of Israel. Even as he has put you down, you, the mighty prince, now a lowly servant, our sovereign has made the girl a slave."

"You speak of the peaceful princess? Avishag, the shepherdess?"

"I speak of the daughter of Salem. Did not even the

Father of Multitudes bow before Melchizedek the King of Peace? Did not all godly men give him tithes? Yet, what great acclaim would one man gain, should he have a tenth of such a woman's fame?"

"Avishag, the daughter of shepherd kings and potent priests. She is choice. Gentle are her feet upon the earth, and her subtle voice through the air. Clever are her words, and kind her works. Yea, and how blessed would I be, if she would love me? Tenfold more blessed than any man. Whose reward exceeds his whose wife may raise royal brood? Yet, still he scoffs, Solomon the Fool."

So says Abiathar, "Look how the elders hide their thoughts from Solomon. See how they bow their heads in anger. Bearing the heirs of David, an Egyptian wounds Israel. Solomon lies in bed with Israel's oppressor. Uplift the elders. Be a savior for Zion. Marry Avishag. Win the favor of a queen the people love. For none but a true king should possess such a queen."

"How shall I marry her or any other of the king's harem? Steal her away secretly? All the women of Solomon flock together like birds of the air. When one turns, so do the others. When one takes flight, the rest follow. I shall be seen as a hawk among the doves. I will be stoned to death by the slings of the watchmen."

Abiathar, knowing Adonijah would thus question him, answers, "Prince, do you not trust me? Believe you that I would lead you to destruction; to be food for the beasts of the field and the birds of the air? I have spied for you the loveliest of Israel's doves. Look! Even now, she coos alone at the doors of the Tent of the Lord."

"I pray you, do not tempt me, Priest. I am weak with envy, but I would be a good servant to my brother. Lead me not on deadly paths, for what woman would a man not kill for? For what queen would man not go to war? I would live to a leathered age if I may but walk softly through my days."

* * *

Adonijah does go to Avishag, and she says, "As the ram runs to the bleating lamb, so Adonijah cannot stay himself from my aid. He comes to me, even as a friend who would uplift a fallen fellow.

"Behold how Adonijah does love me. As a shepherd loves a lamb, so Adonijah loves me, the shepherdess. With tender kisses and loving caress, he cares for me. And I turn to his hand, like a flower seeks the sun. He is as a downy nest for which to lay my head. To Adonijah, I am the dover's favorite turtle, and the prince preens me as a princess, as a cob his cygnet. I lamented as the mourning bird. I sang unheard as the mute swan does sing, but as brazen bells ring, so with each tear Adonijah's heart rang to heal me. Now, I am joyous as the diving duckling, and he as proud as the raucous drake. He would keep me from harm, and give to me happiness."

She feels all this.

Yet... Hear, oh Adonijah, hear the spirit's warning. Heed that dark foreboding. Jealous is a man engaged. Beware your younger brother, who may yet encase you in chains, or like a lion rend you, that your veins be drained of blood, and your heart not beat again.

Chapter 11:
Torn

The Elders congregate to counsel, like crows to fresh sown corn. Abiathar stands among them, speaking, a saboteur sowing tares.

"Solomon has turned his feet aside and brought Israel down a path crooked and cluttered, broad and bewildering. Solomon has despised the daughters of Israel and wed an outsider. Seductive is the bait of a trap, and the hand of he who clings to it shall be cut off! Let us not follow in folly. Let us not trust in treason. But let us go where bright light shines, and wisdom is guided by tradition. Let Adonijah be our guide, he who will vouchsafe our virtues."

As Abiathar speaks, so many have thought, and many heads now nod.

One young and curly speaks, "Does not the Law command, does it not advise that sons of Israel should not take foreign wives. Let us not be led astray, for the Lord's way is strait. Let us not take crooked paths nor forked roads to foreign daughters."

An elder, wise and gray, speaks and says, "Speak not against the Lord's anointed. Have not mighty men loved strange women? Did not our redeemers do as Solomon? Moses an Ethiopian. Joseph an Egyptian."

"Yes!" the crowd does chorus.

"Abiathar, your fealty is fickle, your confessions are crooked, but Solomon's path is straight. With blocks he builds the House of God, and you would lay a street of stumbling stones. He works the will of Jah, but your speech is disease."

* * *

Adonijah goes before Bathsheba, kneels before his father's queen.

She asks, "Are you come in peace or violence?"

And he answers, "I am come in peace, a humble man in love. I grovel as the dog, my throat exposed. I tremble at my brother's words, and quake to contemplate my death. Yet I risk all for she who deserves all gifts, she who is in every way perfect."

"From such a man I fear humility. Reach to touch such a one, and he will turn again to bite me. Who of my house is so lovely that man would face horrid death?"

"Avishag, the Salemite. She is so fair as to make death seem bright to dark life without her. Where she walks, other women seem like long shadows cast."

"Deadly are your desires, Adonijah. A grave gift you ask of me, a gift I cannot grant. You speak of treason!"

"Speak not of treason, nor past hatred. Let my brother make peace with me. Let me find love in my heart for the brother that spared me, though he takes from me my birthright. Let me be a loyal friend, and never raise my hand against him, though he may yet slay me. Though I walk in fear upon the land of my fathers, I must speak of love. Perhaps there is some love for me in Solomon's heart, for I would have Avishag to wife, if he would but give her. But he will never give her if I ask. This I know. But with tender words you may soften my brother's heart. Speak my love into his ears that he might hearken unto them. He will not refuse you."

* * *

Jerusalem, look out from the city. Smoke roils from kindled pyres, a savor sent up to foreign gods. Pharaoh's daughter and Pharaoh's priests ride out to the river to worship. On the hills round about the Holy City, fires and fleshy feasts mock Moses' Law.

* * *

Like waters to a pit, the elders flow to Abiathar and Joab. Abiathar casts his words, to gather men as fish.

"Let no one now say, 'Abiathar has spoken wrong,' nor 'Abiathar has laid a stone on which to stumble in our path.' See now that all that was said has now been done. Will we procrastinate, waiting for the perversion of our Promised Land? Should Israel thirst forever because Solomon lets the gentiles crouch to defile the pure running waters of Jerusalem? You all know that the kingdom was Adonijah's. Israel chanted his name as king, but now the kingdom has turned away, and you have all become Solomon's. So say you, 'The kingdom is his from the Lord.' Yet, now blazing offerings burn about Jerusalem to the baalim of Egypt! Join me. Let us anoint he who has done no deeds to detain him from the seat of kings. God's will be done!"

The men murmur.

Joab stands above the elders. "Let all distraught stay! Rage! Lay waste to the profane! Let all who would stand against us go. Cursed be those who oppose the rightfully anointed of God!"

All stay, for all of them are the discontented of the city. All that are content do not seek a king, for they have a king in Solomon.

"Rally your houses," yells Joab. "Rally your kinsmen and sons. Tomorrow we will stand before the gates of Jerusalem; a mighty wave to sweep away the reek of Egypt and the false king who bows to unknown gods!"

* * *

Adonijah grieving dons his greaves, contemplates his life of violence, longs for one of peace. So speaks Adonijah, the firstborn son of Haggith,

"To fly. To flee the home of my father... But Abiathar has rallied the men to war. I would hide in the hallowed hills of the wilderness, seek out the darkness where no man goes, but Solomon will seek me. Should I stay, death may find me."

Adonijah runs through the city, takes wing up the stairs to his brother's harem.

"Avishag, come away with me. Be a symbol to the land of a pure rule. Stand upon the hill of sacrifice with me, and burn lambs to the most high God, that we may sit upon the throne together as wife and lord. Come away with me, that I may know the Lord is pleased with me, for if one so righteous stands with us, who can be against us?"

The women of the harem beat at the rebel son of David, as geese beat the osprey come to steal a gosling. They pull his hair and tear his skin as teasers catch and part the wool of sheep.

"Come away with me, most peaceful child of my father's harem. Come away and love me."

Avishag cries out, and holds to Adonijah, who is her heart. Like the babe pulled between two mothers, she cries out. Her seamless robe tears and parts like wool shorn by shears. So this day her soul is rent.

Bathsheba scorns her husband's son, "I thought you a man changed, but you are ever full of envy, ever seeking to be the sun when night follows your every step. You shall go down to death this day, never again to molest nor make afraid, and not a single tear shall be shed upon your sinner's grave. David's hairs were grey with sorrow for his sons Absolom and Adonijah, and I cry these last tears on your youthful head, but the world shall no more mourn for the wickedness of my beloved's sons!"

Chapter 12:
Birds of the Air

Solomon is at his ease, gay in leisure, laughing and without worry. Bathsheba enters his hall. She bows to her son the king. Solomon stands and bows.

"My lord, I request a private audience of you. Send out your friends, release your guards, for my words are sharp and must find your heart."

Solomon sends his servants away and his guests are guided out.

"Speak mother. What troubles you?"

Bathsheba weeps and holds out the spoiled garment of Avishag. "Adonijah has defiled your harem. He has come as a snake to steal eggs, and has demanded Avishag for his wife."

Solomon's brow is furrowed. He takes the cloth in his hands and sees that the coat is the garment he gave to Avishag for a gift. He groans from his belly, falls. "How I have hated wisdom and scorned reproof. God do worse to me and more if Adonijah has not done this thing against his own life."

Benaiah knocks at the door. Solomon permits him to enter. The captain bows to his lord.

"Lord, Adonijah is without the city. An army is without the gates, blusterous as a storm, numerous as the dust, ready to turn our city red!"

Solomon rends his shirt and screams, "As the Lord lives, Adonijah shall die this day!"

* * *

Adonijah joins Joab and the discontented horde. They march upon the city. A dark cloud looming, they approach the city. Adonijah glistens in his plated armor and polished greaves. The throng engulfs the western wall as a hawk hovers, mantles its prey.

And Adonijah says to his gathered men, "I look out upon the fields and see my loyal brethren aligned to battle for their chosen king. I weep. My station has been stolen from me. I seek peace with my brother, but the world conspires against me. Now, battle is my only chance to live. While in peace I must surely die, rather let me grasp the sword and reign. The brother in times past I would have killed with jealous ire, I now sorrowfully take up my buckler against. For me, there may be no repentance to him who gave me but a single chance. Our brotherhood is shattered like a pot, and the precious care inside flows out upon the dust. I cry, and the ground drinks my tears, as it shall the blood of Israel this day. Either he or I must die, and many more besides. And the Lord is not to be found to save me, nor a prophet in the land to speak refrain to David's son, the king."

In a chariot the usurper flies from among the men; drives to the gate alone. "Open your gates Jerusalem! Open your gates, that your rightful king may sit upon his throne!"

The gates open.

Leather pouch and woolen string give flight to murderous

stone. Cracking the prince's perfect pate, a lifeless rock brings an end to life's lovely breaths. Adonijah's helmet falls, and blood trickles down his arched brow. Woozy, he slips and stoops upon his hands and knees, low in the dust. His men stand stupefied, deaf and dumb. From wall nor field, no caw nor whistle breaks the silence of the maddened crowds.

Benaiah strides across the empty space, grips the prince's black plaited braids, and slits the smooth pillar of his throat. Like a spring that feeds the luscious green fields, blood flows forth to wet the thirsty soil. And Adonijah crumples, a shriveled plant within the desert between two armies, his strength wilting before Benaiah's heated wrath.

Like beating wings, men's feet throw dust. As birds of the air the men take flight. When one turns, so do the others, and Adonijah lays stoned to death by the watchmen, like a hawk among the doves.

Joab fastest flies and finds his way through the gates to the tabernacle. Gripped with terror, he grabs the altar's horns. Benaiah, like an eagle, spots the frightened man. Solomon follows and sees as well.

Benaiah calls out to the captain of hosts, "So says the king, 'Come out from the Tent of the Lord. Desecrate the house of David no more.'"

"No! I will die here!" the conspirator crows from within the tent, the traitor.

The king commands Benaiah, "Do as he has said and fall upon him. Bury him, and the Lord shall return upon his head the blood of the innocents he has shed, even Abner and Amasa; far better men than he."

Benaiah does as he is told, swords and spears his talons. Joab is seized and slain in the House of God. He shall be buried beneath a mound of stones out in the wilderness. His sins shall be buried without the city, that the throne of David will have peace from him forever.

* * *

Abiathar is found mourning atop a hill. His clothes are torn and his hair sullied with dirt. A man condemned, he is brought before the king.

Solomon says to Abiathar, "Because you were a friend to my father through all his afflictions when many were his enemies and few his allies; because you have borne the Ark of God, and God has not smitten you down, I will spare you. You deserve death. Return to your fields, but do not return to Jerusalem. You are thrust out."

So it is that the Lord's word is fulfilled concerning the house of Eli. So it is that Abner and Amasa are avenged. So it is that Solomon is established upon the throne of David.

Chapter 13:
Ascending to the Throne

Night descends over Jerusalem. Bathsheba bows low to Solomon who sits in private contemplation, pondering the judgment of Avishag. The queen mother kisses her son's feet, "Lord, do not harm the girl. She was overcome by a moment's passion. She is yet a virgin."

Solomon stands and pushes his mother away. "How can I know, when her feelings are so cloaked, and the truth is darkly shrouded? The maidservant has many times seen Avishag open her door to my brother. Avishag made no outcry that she might be rescued. She has been as silent as a cloud, as furtive as a vapor. If my brother has known her, the Law commands that she be stoned without the city gate!"

Bathsheba clutches at the robes of her son. "So says the law of justice, but what of the law of mercy? Is our god not a merciful god as well as a just? I beg you to spare her. She can be sworn to silence. No one will know if she was defiled."

"As a free man, I might be allowed mercy. As a king, I must exact the Law."

"My son, the Lord is the King of Kings, the Lord of Lords and yet he is merciful. Please my son, show kindness. Do not kill the child. Judge her not by the appearance of sin, but rather by her heart which is pure."

"I will not judge her today. Put her away privately somewhere. Do not let her speak to anyone but you. I need time to know what is wise. Only the Lord's scale is just. Only the Lord knows the weight in each scale, whether it will lean to righteousness or deceit."

Bathsheba went and did as she was commanded.

* * *

Nathan next comes to visit the king. Solomon is in grief, stirring his mind to understanding, seeking to know wisdom.

"Tell me, Nathan, what must I do?"

"You are not blameless, Solomon. You have let foreign gods be worshipped in the sacred land of the Lord. When you should have been like the sun and the cool breeze of morning, Adonijah has come, like the darkness of night, when the stars are blotted out and the smoke of burning fields chokes the air. Cleanse yourself, and like the sun, rise up tomorrow and go west with your priests and elders. All of you sacrifice the best of the flocks to the Lord God of Israel, that your gratitude might be known, and that the land might be cleansed of the iniquity that pollutes our people. When the sun rests at the closing of the day, so shall you rest. Ask the Lord what must be done. Do not trust your heart of flesh to know what is good and evil. Rather, trust in God."

* * *

The sun rises in the east. Solomon travels with the priests to Gibeon. Thousands follow in the caravan. King, clergy, cattle and countrymen hike the heights of the hilly-city, that a great sacrifice might be offered to the Lord God of Israel, who has been merciful to Jerusalem, that no blameless man died for the sake of the usurpers.

Upon the greatest mount of Gibeon, Solomon burns incense, and sacrifices one thousand burnt offerings to the Lord. Goats die, that God might know man's gratitude.

The blood's embrace is warm. The king's clothes clutch his stomach, steaming. His sandals, slick, stick to his feet, red with sanguine muck. He stands justified in carnage, purified by perfumed smoke.

Solomon says, "Can man stand blameless in so much blood? Can wool again be white after what I have sacrificed to be made king?"

The slaughter is done.

He washes in a clear running stream, and goes off alone, cleansed. He rests his head upon sheeps' skins, and sleeps.

A roaring whirlwind fills his ears. The pounding of drums and the rush of voices echo in his head. A voice cries out his name. His door shutters as if banged. He rises out of bed, shocked awake.

A raucous crowd riots outside his door. He cleanses with clear cold water, clothes himself in a seamless coat of pure white wool. Barefooted, he walks out to the judgment hall.

The people hiss and move like wheat blowing in the wind. He parts the mob like the farmer parts the tall grasses of his fertile fields. Avishag cowers amidst them all, quivering like a dappled fawn. All around her, men raise stones, poised to crush and shatter her frail form. Solomon tries to push through the crowd to save her. He cries out. Men and women beset him with charges, and an outcry for justice. They peck and point, a murder of crows to persecute Avishag. She sobs for mercy. The people swell against Solomon like a wave.

His head hangs low. He stumbles, and they tear at him. They rend his robe. He pushes through his assailants; makes his way slowly to the steps of his throne. The steps rise above him; a mountain of stone. He peers down upon his subjects. They swarm like ants below his feet, Avishag miniscule, a grain of sand. He looks again to his throne, set so high beyond his sight, a lofty mountainous height. He climbs. Blood streams down the stairs, immersing his feet, splashing his garment. His brothers lay dead, corpses on the cathedra's steps. Wounds agape, scarlet rivers flow from each gashed neck. His brothers' blood turns his clothing red. He mourns over their torn bodies, holds them, kisses each its fair and perfect face.

A great fire burns below. It will consume him, he knows. He leaves his brothers' bodies and climbs higher. The smoke is a billowing cloud that veils the throne. Resinous odors of coniferous saps spice the smothering smog. The choking curtain sears his eyes and floods his panting lungs. He is overcome, clamoring for breath above the clouds.

"Hear, O Lord! I am in distress! Hear me Lord! Deliver me! Hear me, God, that I do not die!"

A light shines in the darkness. Solomon is seized, and as the archer's string casts its shaft, he is flown to the throne of thrones. He lays crumpled, dumb, stunned as if to death.

"Stand, you king of Israel."

Solomon covers his face. "Lord! I beg you. Your wrath has been hard upon my soul. I cannot stand against the battering waves of mine enemies. I have sought comfort with my friends but have found no love in them."

"STAND! You king of Israel!"

Solomon trembles. His legs are water. "I cannot Lord. I am as one who has been laid in the grave."

"STAND! YOU KING OF ISRAEL!" The Lord grips Solomon; powerful, piercing as the lion's clenching claws.

Solomon stands and weeps, embraced in the mighty bosom of the mightiest God.

Chapter 14: Wisdom

The Lord points, "Look, man."

Solomon looks. The smoke and mist part, and the sun shines through as at noon. Solomon raises his hands to shield himself from the glory of the day.

Again the Lord speaks, "Look, Solomon."

Solomon looks out from the mountain and sees the land below, all the country promised to his fathers and beyond, to all the world.

"All of this is mine, Solomon. I may give it to you, if you ask."

Solomon stares out into the vast world. He sees incomprehensible wealth; flocks without number, orchards weighed down, boughs bent with unaccountable bounty, flowing veins of minerals deep in the earth. The sight of it tempts him.

Solomon stares again and sees the wool of the flocks, that it is corrupted by moths, that the fruits fall to the earth and are spoiled. He sees too his death, and that all his riches are divided.

"Vanity," says Solomon. "I see now that a man may toil for riches all his days under the sun, and yet has not gained."

The Lord points again, "Look."

Solomon looks. He sees those around him, his beloved family, ashen and aging; whilst he remains beautiful, young and golden.

"You may have long life Solomon. I can give you this too, if you ask."

Solomon looks out upon the world and sees that the rivers flow from the mountains down to the sea, and yet the sea is never satisfied. He sees generations of men born, red faced, loved and bloody, and die, pale and lonely.

"This too is vanity, for man's longings will never cease. Mine eyes will never be satisfied by looking, nor will mine ears cease longing to hear. I see that mortality must find all things, and man is not exempt from the corruption of time."

"See Solomon that your enemies surround you round about! Hear them crying out for the shedding of Israel's blood! Smell the smoke of their sacrifices to false gods! Does this not rile you to anger? Do you not wish to blot them out? Destroy them forever, and you shall have peace the remaining years of your life. I can give you this, if you ask."

Solomon looks out upon the fields of war; armies regaled in armor, the glistening oiled shields, the shining of spears, the shouting voices, the thundering feet. Then, all turns gloomy. The sun burns as a glowing coal in the sky, its never ending fires cease. Solomon falls to the ground and weeps. Blood and bodies spread across the dusty earth. Women and children moan. Men cry and kiss their battered brothers.

"No, Lord, I do not desire this."

"Ask what you will, and it will be yours."

"You have been kind to my father, inasmuch as he has walked before you in righteousness. You have blessed him greatly, in that you have placed his son upon the throne of Israel to rule a great multitude; a people so great they cannot be numbered. But I am only a youth. I do not know how to live the life given me. I ask of you, Lord, that you give your servant an understanding and compassionate heart, so that I may be able to discern good from evil, and judge this mighty people righteously."

The Lord smiles on Solomon. "Because you have asked for wisdom and not for the destruction of your enemies, long life, nor riches, I have given you even as you have desired. I have also given what I desire for you, riches and honor. There will be no king like you as long as you live. If you live as your father, walking in the light of the understanding that I have shone upon you, your days will be lengthened. Now come, be clean. Though your sins be as scarlet, you shall be as innocent as a lamb, as white as the fallen snow."

The Lord leads Solomon to a basin of water set deep in the stone. Solomon removes his blood-sullied garment, and steps into the water with the Lord. The water draws from him all the blood of his brothers. The Lord dips him beneath the water, pushes him into darkness and nothing.

Solomon awakens, as though he fell into waking.

He rises and leaves Gibeon before his men, and walks to the tabernacle in Jerusalem. He burns incense before the Ark of the Covenant. He burns a sacrifice to God, and gives offerings of peace to the Lord. He feasts with all his servants and the people of his house. All celebrate in the glory of their king.

All but Avishag, who fears her fate, alone.

Chapter 15: Banished

Avishag, blessed little dove, how the world has scorned you. How the world has conspired against you, and turned love into death.

Oh daughters of Jerusalem, look to Avishag. Remember her when the passionate sap of youth wells in your trunks. Remember, do not wake love before its time.

She lies in the darkness, quaking scared, frightened of her fate.

Avishag, look not to man to save you, but rather to God, for man has brought you to this frightful place, and bestowed you with fears. With God, all loves are pure, and none corrupt. But with man, love is captured and caged, cravings held at ransom to keep men bound.

Breathe deep. Do not fear death. No longer draw tearful, croaking breaths.

Avishag, you are right with the Lord, and he will deliver you. He loves you, though loneliness is your allotment.

* * *

Avishag is given to her brother's care. She is banished from Solomon's Jerusalem.

"Oh blessed little sister, whom we cherish, we will send you home, and all our wealth and all our gold will be garnered to see that you will not perish, a poor maiden, alone and impoverished. Brothers are born to bear the burdens of their sisters' griefs.

"Guard our father's gardens. Make rich the vines that yield red wine. Be at rest in the Lands of Peace."

The brothers hold and kiss her, and cry many tears, knowing what is done to her.

And when the three called the Jubaalim are alone, they speak candidly without guard.

"What has been done is not right; for spoiled princes to so ruin an innocent's life. Were Adonijah still alive, I'd, with my hammer, split his face, and bury him in an unmarked grave."

Chapter 16: Home

Avishag, Bathsheba has not forgotten you. She has remembered her promise unto David, who was a father unto you. Bathsheba has allotted you an inheritance in Sharon. She has made you a wealthy woman in the land of Salem. You are blessed, and blessings are ever on your lips for Bathsheba's sake, mother of the king who has forsaken you.

Make the land rich. Give your elders good food that they might stand straight. Give your maidens labors that they wane not into weakness. Give your boys flocks that they might feed their many houses and age bravely into manhood, facing the night with courage and their foes with rage. The day will come when men say of you, she was a lady wise, and all who served her loved her.

But remember, Avishag, wake not love until it is time. You are a woman alone, and may love no man but Solomon.

Chapter 17:
The Traveler

Avishag's boys, bold and broad are now turned to men; their flocks span the plains of Sharon. Her maidens' hands are clever. Their tapestries are treasures. Her old men are lithe and lean. And all say, "We love our lady."

Avishag returns from her labors.

Beneath the olive's boughs, beside the stony well, sits a traveler. In the late day's shade sits a man whose beauty is beyond even those born of beloved David's loins. She draws him water, and he slakes his thirsty tongue.

"From whence have you come, traveler; and whither are you going?"

"From east to west, and west to east again. I have seen your land, and stranger though I am, have said to myself, I will go there, and meet the lady so loved by all who serve her. Seeing you, I am blessed, as was Jacob, and I long to kiss you, for your beauty is beyond that of the sisters of Solomon."

Avishag hides her face, but her maidens blush and will not turn away.

"Let him eat with us. Let him stay in the fields, that we may look upon him."

"Foreigner, would you sup with us? Stranger, will you sleep in our fields?"

"My every minute is measured, my every hour set upon the gauge. My work is not finished, but when it is done, I will dine with you, and work in the fields, that I might show gratitude where you have shown grace."

The Traveler

* * *

At dusk each day, the traveler comes to rest at the roots of the twisted tree that overhangs the straight walled rocky well. He jovially speaks with each shepherd there, drinks and prepares for his next day of labors. He fills his sack with water, and the laborers with laughter.

Sabbath has come, and time to rest.

The maidens beg their mistress, "Send for him, Avishag, that he might feast with us, and that we may look upon his lovely face."

She beckons a boy. "Go little child. Find the man we all love. Find Hiram. If you know not where he rests, follow the sheep to the shepherds' tents. There you will find him."

The child bids him welcome, and he comes to break bread with Avi's home, for she is rich with meats and fruits, rich with monies and fabricked clothes. Hiram dips his sop with the humble servants, and gawks in awe at this woman, the mistress of her own abode, the master in command of many men.

Yet, Avishag is shocked by this workman. His brazen stare has made her tongue a caged bird. Her throat is closed to hold it, and she cannot speak. He looks upon her as though she is his wife, and not the lone mistress of her own great house; as if he is the father of the many children, ruddy cheeked and chubby; master of the many men, straight and strong; and lover of every lady, luscious and young.

She frees the words held within her ribs. "Hiram, set aside hard stones and dark iron chisels. Come tomorrow. Sheer soft sheep and wash them white with us."

"If my mistress wishes, I will work in the washing pools with the shepherds."

"Yes, Master Hiram, I wish it."

Chapter 18:
Washing Pools and Fir Bowers

Come down, Hiram! Come down to the washing pools. The morning sun has shone on the dusty lambs ready to be shorn, and the edges of the shepherds' sheers glisten, waiting for the wool-rich sheep.

Hiram wakes, and each day works to tend the flocks of Avishag. Women gather wool in sacks, later to be cleansed. Hiram girds his loins and goes down to the water shirtless, his stomach strongly formed like smooth sapphires set in reddened clay, his chest like golden tablets, and legs of sturdy marble stone set in silver sockets. And Avishag longs for Hiram, as the spinner for her yarn, or the mason's hands the solid stone.

* * *

The sun beams from meridian height, and Hiram prays among the shadows of the orchard. Surrounded by nettles, he kneels among the lilies. The wild grass receives his naked knees.

From the coolness of the olive press, Avishag stares, silently secreted within the dark and shaded stairs. Shrinking, scared, she slips. Her feet slap the stones, and Hiram, startled, turns to see who hides, to see she who secretly spies.

"Dove, hidden in the stony press, I have heard your wings beat your breasts. Let me see your face. Let me hear your voice."

From the darkness, Avishag is revealed, and light shines upon her even features, golden as the wheaten fields.

"Truly, you have dove's eyes... and your voice I know is sweet."

Avi's chest is a marching force. She is struck. Fear floods her blood like an army's waving banners.

Hiram approaches. "Your temples are as pomegranates, your face as flushed as the river after rain."

She shields her face. Sheltered in her shawl, her feathered hair drapes her ruddy cheeks. "Turn from me, Hiram. Your eyes overcome me, and I am terrified."

He reaches, and her hair accepts his touch. "Please, do not hide your face, nor shroud your beauty with black locks. I look upon you as one who cannot turn away. Like a man in the desert, I have seen a tree and have said to myself, 'I will go up and run my hands through the leaves of it.'"

"Shade and comfort I may give, but do not ask for love."

"It is my heart needs comfort, not my body, for could I not lie beneath a tree when the sun is at its most violent heat, and yet be shielded. But I do battle with the noon, that I might be near you. And that my longing might be assuaged, many a man awaits his wage. I tarry and postpone their pay, only in hopes that I might hold you."

"When the shadows lengthen in the fields, and the day's work is finished, find me in the forest. For I too am feint with love and would have you meet me again within the grove."

* * *

AVISHAG

Avishag fears the beautiful man hidden in the dark woods. The sun lies upon the earth, and the shadows embrace the entire world, and yet, Avi enters the grove, brushing her hands along the smooth gnarled knots of the ancient trunks. The air is thick with quince and conifer. A mist does kiss the green grass with dew; and Hiram lies alone in the darkened wood.

"Come," he says. "Partake. The wine is delicious to the taste and very desirable."

They stay their thirst with flagons, and drink to temptation. They laugh and sing; their voices like the gently purring turtle-doves'; drinking joy as only lovers pour, speaking words that only lovers know.

"The night is come," she says, "and I should be home, sheltered from the darkening gloom."

But Hiram lies down, and casts his eyes toward the speckled sky. "Stay. What are stone built houses to the garden home made by God? Here, our bed is green, cedars are our beams, and fir our rafters. Fear not the moonless night, for the Lord says, 'let there be light,' and the canopy of heaven drapes us like a shawl of lamp lit cities. What need have we for the comforts of men?"

Avi lies beside her swain, and Hiram hovers o'er her like dark clouds full of rain, so that through him, not a single star might be seen. And she lies beneath him, as a field freshly tilled and sown with seed.

"With fear and trembling, I embrace you, yet I lay beneath your shadow with great delight, and trust your love is sweet."

And she sweetly bleeds, as does the myrrh its sap.

Chapter 19:
King's Errand

Go now, Hiram, to the King of Tyre. Every mason is worth his due, every man owed his wage. Go to Hurim, King of Tyre, whose wealth is equal to his works, his harbors and canals flowing rich with merchant ships upon the waters. Go now to Lebanon's king, where the forests scratch the skies with their godly stems. Go where is sold the sweetest spices from every port that touches ocean, and where is sold the softest wool of Kedar's silken flocks. Go to collect the coins of copper, silver, and gold, and the many gems ingeniously wrought by masters' hands. Gather you the riches the king commends to your care, that all the craft be paid their share.

Go to the king. Report. Let him know what his generous soul has bought. Tell him of the gleaming temple on Moriah's mount, where God will descend and sit his throne. Tell him of the pillars, made not of stone but stalwart bronze; the twins Jachin and Boaz, erected in strength and dedicated to God.

And return swiftly to Jerusalem, guarded with the strong and mighty men assigned you by the benevolent Warden, Hurim, King of Tyre. Turn neither to the left nor the right. Return not to Sharon, for there a love is awakened that is meant to sleep.

Chapter 20:
The Proposition

Avishag, look out from the hilltop. Who is it that comes out of the desert like a proud pillar of smoke, with all the trappings and powders of the merchants and many valiant men surrounding him? Behold, it is Hiram, like a stag, leaping over the walls, skipping up the hills to find you. Behold, he stands at your door full of happiness, peering through the lattice, and peeking in the windows.

Hiram speeds like a buck to Avishag. "Arise Avi! Arise my fair one and follow me. The birds are chirping. The doves are cooing. The winter is past! Arise and come away!"

Avi follows hand in hand with Hiram. Delighted, she follows him to her home where stands a line of men with gifts, fabrics, oils, spices most delicious. Hiram kisses his doe-eyed mate, lays before his beloved the wealth he has saved, gilds her neck like a tower gird with gold and silver shields, an homage in hopes of marriage.

"Come with me to Jerusalem and we will be wed. Be near to my heart, a rib in my chest, never to be separate."

Avi weeps and clings to Hiram. "Let us leave. Let us flee, like roe and hind, and live together. Let us leave all behind, and be as doves among the wild cliffs where none will find, and none molest!"

Hiram stands stunned. "No Avi. Why do you speak of fleeing? Come away with me to Solomon in the City of Peace, Jerusalem! Let us live in wealth, with deep wells, lovely orchards, and mountains of herbs."

Avi's passions swell. Like an old skin that holds new wine, she bursts with lamentations. "You will not flee with me, and I cannot come with you. I must stay – a flower without a bee, untouched in the valley of Sharon."

Hiram, distressed, clutches her closely to his breast. "Will you not then cling to me, as I would cleave to you?"

"I would, yet cannot. Please Hiram, leave. Marry one or the many women more worthy, for you are a man of greatest worth; the best I've ever known."

Hiram's hope is blown out. He is a lamp without oil, or a naked wick without wax. Like the wafting of smoke, he returns to his camp, and cries.

Chapter 21:
Searching for Love

Avi seeks Hiram in her restless dreams. In her sleep, she lifts her airy form. She leaves her bed to seek her love in the city of Jerusalem. She seeks him in the broad roads, and the narrow alleys, the nocturnal doorways, and the night's shadowed corners. She longs for her lover but finds him not.

The guards of the city gather 'round her, ready to guide her home.

She says, "Have you seen Hiram, whom I love?"

"We have not, but whispers hide in every stone, ready to anger, and murder those who roam the night seeking fleeting love. Go, and do not wake until it's dawn."

Only briefly has she passed the city's watchmen and she finds the sojourner she so loves. She enfolds him in her fervent clutch and will not let him go. She leads him into her mother's home, their house at Jerusalem, into the chamber of she that conceived her – and awakens.

Still is the night. The moon is high, full and bright. The streaming light casts shaped shade upon her bed.

Avi stands and stares out the latticed stones. She sees Hiram there by the well; not a dream nor a specter, but a man of flesh and bone standing in the fog. She fears to trust the yearnings that draw her near her waiting hart.

"Never has a man enclosed my love so dearly in his hands. Never have I brought a lover to my bed."

She goes to him, and pining, holds him.

"What dreams I've had. Nightly I walk the streets to

hold your ghastly form; and when I wake, risen with the light of dawn, you are gone, and I mourn the empty space between my arms. I would have you run, but this night, I will have you lay your head to sleep upon my breathing bosom."

In through the door she leads, into the bed her father made.

Hiram's hands shape her sloping legs, as with the grace of his craft.

"How supple are your feet, and slender your ankles, let them be unshod. A prince's daughter has not such a lovely foot. Your thighs are polished stone, pillars to adorn the temple of your form, the work of God's hands, a cunning workman.

"Your belly is a mound of wheat fresh from the threshing floor, smooth and shining. And your breasts, soft as fur, are warm as fawns huddled sleeping.

"Your lips drip with spikenard, and each kiss smells of quince."

With his left hand Hiram holds her head. With his right he does embrace her.

* * *

Lo, arises the morning sun, and Avishag implores her lovely maidens, "Do not stir up nor wake my love until he pleases."

She knows, when he awakens, he will away.

Chapter 22:
The Temple and the Grove

The temple stands nearly finished. Jewels flash and gold glistens, lying in piles where the master jewelers await commissions. At the temple door, erect, the brazen pillars have been set, and incense wafts its savory scent up to Heaven. Chanting priests, clashing cymbals, tinkling chimes and singing women please the ears of every person.

"Holiness to the Lord, His home is a pleasure to all souls, and an homage to Solomon."

"Surely, the Lord has blessed Hiram; his hands more clever than any man's, his spirit endued with greater genius. God's love for Hiram endures forever!"

* * *

Heaps of wheat, horns of oil, sacks of wine; the brethren arrive to receive their dues. There is one among them who has given his token falsely, sought to garner what goods he has not earned. A fellowcraft, he thought he knew the master's word, thought he knew a master's grip.

Hiram, through the lattice, grips the traitor's wrist, pulls his face against the stone.

Lo, the Ruffians, men of Shulem but called the Jubaalim of Tyre, grab the man and drag him from the wall where Hiram stands concealed behind the stones. The frenzied craft shout curses, shift and crowd. Their fists beat hard on the imposter, smashing down upon his head and ribs. And the brothers thrust him to the block.

"What says our master? What is just? What punishment for the impersonator who would steal from us?"

Hiram speaks, "Seize upon the man. Grip him hard, that he may not hie away. Hold him down, and strike off his hand."

The accused cries out, "Brethren! Is there not one among you who will speak for me? For are we not all underpaid? Are we not all hungry?"

Yet, none come to speak on his behalf.

The strongest of the Jubaalim holds up his curving sword, and swiftly severs the thief's stealing arm.

Blood beads like quicksilver in the sand, pouring profusely from the man's severed hand.

The thief cries out, "Curses and death upon you, Master Hiram! For all men sin, but you have sinned against your friends. We who have loved you starve, and yet erect your marvelous plans. By these hands was this temple raised, and what paltry meals have been our pay, and what harsh retribution for seeking to be on the level with our better skilled brethren."

Hiram answers with anger, "You are as one who snapping takes, like a dog fit only to be stricken. Like the jackal at the lion's kill, you slyly came, but were bitten. You have taken with the left what I have given with the right. You have deceived me; I, who would be your friend, and you would label me the fiend. Take not those dues that are not yours, lest your friends turn again and rend you!"

The eldest ruffian steps forth, he speaks for all the men of Shulem. "Brother Hiram, this man has come as the jackal snapping, but we like the lions have been waiting. We wish too to have the lions share. When will we get the wages that were promised long ago? When will we be made masters, to work at home or abroad? We are kept here like servants, hardly slaves, though slaves to God's great majesty. We would not complain, except that we have waited so patiently."

"Craftsmen, this is neither the time nor the place. Wait until the temple is completed, then if you are found worthy, you shall all be raised as masters and receive masters' wages, otherwise you shall not."

The punished man yells from his place in the dirt. "Talk not to me of time nor place. Now is the time of want. Here is the place of subjugation. It is not right that we have toiled and are yet found unworthy. God will weigh you in his scales, Master Hiram, and like all men, you will be found wanting."

* * *

Avishag's servants clear the groves of briars and the fields of tares. They are upon Hiram's place of prayer, the ancient olive grove and the aged olive press. The trees are barren, or the fruits are bitter. The branches shoot in wild sprouts reaching for the sun. The laborers hack the olives down, burn the briars and make the grove a field for seeds, barren dirt ready to be sown.

The fire eats; all its refuse turned to ash. The earth burns black, and brambles brown and green crackle in the heat.

Avishag walks through the grove. She holds her shawl that it will not be snagged. She peers to Hiram's haunt, a sunlit bed of grass, nigh invisible through the thorny mass that strangles the struggling trees – there she sees, in a leafy frame, a lonely lily, untouched by flames.

She stares, touched by contemplation, calm within the conflagration.

"Halt your hacking! Smother the smoldering blaze! This grove I will restore; its beauty reinstate."

Chapter 23:
Come up from the Desert

Go forth, daughters of Israel, go forth to Jerusalem! Share in Solomon's great gladness on the day of his marriage. Go forth to see the king ride crowned in his chariot, followed by his men, each one strong, each one valiant. Swarm the streets of Jerusalem, Israel's procession of lovely daughters.

Avishag's maidens cannot be denied, they beg with such feeling to see the sights.

"Take us Avi," they say. "Is not your beloved there? Have we not heard rumors that he saunters in the gardens and lies at night on mountains of spices. Let us go with you, that we may seek your beloved and delight with princes."

They go up to Jerusalem in a fervor, Avishag and her maidens, like a flock of birds chattering in flight.

* * *

Avishag stays in her mother's home, where here brothers sleep in Jerusalem.

Her brothers speak in fear.

"Why have you come to Jerusalem from which you have been banished? Speak to no one and leave."

"Does jealousy and envy drive you, that you must see the king with his chosen queens? Will not your heart rend with longing?"

"Thoughtless girl, have you no care for your family

here? Have you pondered the danger?"

"Hold your reviling tongues," says the mother to her sons. "Avi is yet a lovely dove, yet undefiled in mine eyes. Had she not been forced upon, she would be chieftess among the queens, praised by the concubines, revered by all. She is my singular daughter, the Lord's gifted treasure. Though she is banished from Jerusalem, I am a house standing alone within the city; my daughter may find shelter in my bosom, for the love of a mother triumphs over the command of kings. Now, be silent and go out by the door."

The men turn to leave, but Avi fights further, gnashes at her brothers' backs, "I have come to this leopards cave, this den of lions, not because of envy, though had I a husband, I would love him jealously. I envy the queens only that they may love, while I may not. Curses upon you all, whose judgment is unjust! Curses on you who are free but would subdue your sisters! Curse those who curse me! I who wallow in this cursed fate, ever an exile from man's embrace. Let me have this moment of joy. Let me dally with my sisters in the streets, and for a while forget my woes."

* * *

A river of people flows after Solomon's future wife, fertilizing the city with excitement. Women run after, as if the king's train paves the roads with love. Solomon floats above, in a chariot made of cedar wood, leafed in gold, plated in silver and painted purple.

Following are sixty noble men, bearded and brave,

each man expert in war, everyone a sword on his thigh. In the midst of them, like a cloud of myrrh and frankincense, painted with all the powders of merchants, floats the queen to be, carried by mighty muscled men upon a scarlet-pillowed palanquin.

All work has ceased in the city, the fields and vineyards. Criers go forth shouting joyously, "Go forth you daughters of Zion! Behold Solomon with the crown with which his mother crowned him. Behold him in his day of gladness!"

* * *

Avi watches on in envy – wishing that she too could be celebrated, venerated by her love. The king stands within his chariot, and behind him, a man more beauteous yet rides upon a mule; Hiram. He sees her, one among the throng.

Avishag, he has looked aside, and seen you. Like Moses, he has seen a vision, and will turn aside. You are to him a burning bush, passionately flaming. He must hear you, that he may perceive your thoughts; must speak to the holy illusion you have become, and know why you are not yet consumed with love.

Like smoke in the wind, she disappears, and yet is not gone. She goes to her mother's house and hides herself. Yet, at noon a man knocks.

"Open to me, my love. Open to your traveling man. I have marched, shined upon by burning sun and silver bucklers. My feet are red with dust, and my head is burnt by daylight. Give me rest. Let us repose upon your bed."

"No, I may not open to any man. You must leave, lest my brothers find you and in their ire, smite you. In their anger they will fight to the death. Like battling rams, they will split your head."

"Let them anger," says Hiram, "I am a much greater man than they."

"Than my brothers yes, but you are not greater than those who quarreled for my hand in marriage, nor he to whom I was promised."

"Quarreled? Betrothed? Are both these words not of the past? I will not be bothered. You are to me a boon, but to you, I am distress... Shall I go, and, like a ghost who has passed your thresh, never return again?"

"It is not you that gives distress. Rather, when I see you, my heart takes flight, like the lofty honeybee that alights on the white and yellow buds of the calamus. But to another man I am bound, and my brothers guard me like hounds their house. Hiram, I will never be your spouse. Never know the sounds of your children's laughter, or their feet upon the ground."

"Press your ear against the door, and listen to the words of my lips. Your words make my soul like unto the chariots of Amminadab. My heart beats like the thundering hooves of horses, and my blood rushes through my ears like the wheels of armies. Until the shadows grow too long and creep upon the ground, binding all the world in darkness, I will be alone upon the mountain of frankincense. Get you up to the mountain of spices and meet me there in secret."

***

While yet in the west the setting sun still shines, Avishag climbs the steps to the mountain of spice near Solomon's palace. She finds Hiram there asleep in the orchards. The fragrant sap seeps from slitted bark, and cinnamon trees waft their scent across the breeze.

She dares not wake her love. Rather she watches him breathe, a stag sleeping in his spiced copse; she, his peaceful doe lying dappled in the shade.

The flowers stipple the earth, budding from the green. The singing birds flutter through the leaves, and the turtledoves coo from the tops of trees.

Hiram awakes from his slumber. Waking joy grips him now. He greets Avi with many loving kisses, grasps her in his caring arms.

Speaks Hiram, "When I saw you, I could not first be sure my love stood there, but looking closer, I knew there is no other with such stature. Like a tower of David you stand among the lower peoples, all of them like unto hovels. Your hair, though shawled, cascades down like kashmir herds flowing to your sloping shoulders. Whose teeth but yours shine so bright? White as fresh washed lambs, all twins and none amiss. Who wears such jewels as those I gave you, bucklers of gold and silver studs? You have ravished my heart. I would recognize you by a single eye, or a lone link of the chain I gave you as a gift."

"Oh!" Avi cries, "Oh that others thought you were my brother. Oh that others thought you suckled at the same mother's breasts as I. Then I could find you in the streets, and none would despise; walk with you hand in hand and kiss you. No one would deride a sister's love. I could take you to my mother's house, and there we'd drink spiced wine and the juice of pomegranate. As it is, I must sneak to you, and hide in wild places."

"Darling Sister, my love grows beyond the limits of familiar affection. My spirit cannot release you. Yet, I cannot hold you, as could a brother. My left hand should hold your head, and my right embrace you."

"Let's leave tonight, Hiram. Flee with me to Lebanon. Flee with me from this lions' den. Run away from these leopard spotted mountains."

"Why do you speak so vilely of this garden? My oasis in the desert? Your lips so often drip with words of cream. Comb and honey are your thoughts and deeds. Yet with hatred you now speak of what I love. You ask me to flee a fear I do not know. Yet you will not tell it me. My heart is cleft. Whether I should stay or leave, there is no question. I must stay. I am the great architect of the Temple of the Lord. No greater honor has a craftsman had in all the days of this aging world."

Avishag weeps.

"Please Avishag, if you love me, present yourself tonight as my beloved at the wedding. Solomon will host us gladly. Surely, he will esteem a woman such as you, for you are all that is admirable, all that is beautiful. Will you come?"

Avi's bowels churn with dis-ease. Fear of losing love conquers shame. "Yes, I will come."

Chapter 24:
Dark

Lo, the sun sets. Dressed in a fine wedding stole, Avi steals from her mother's home.

"Oh God, might you be a Lord after my lord David's heart, and love me? Cloak me in your almighty shadow. Let not harsh words harm me, nor spiteful eyes identify me. Grant me the grace of the serpent that is sleek within the grass, silent and unseen. Let me speak to my love in gentle tones, unnoticed, like the cooing of the dusk's final doves, that I wake no suspicion in the king, and incite no shame. Love me, as David loved me. Guard me, as David did guard me."

The women wend through the walkways of the palace, each with their long-wicked lighted lamps full of oil. Avi wends with the rest, a fish in a streaming school of fish. She thinks, *None shall recognize me, one among the many in the teeming sea of guests. Only one who loves as a mother might know me, and none that love me less.*

Within the banquet hall, the high ceilings hang with standards. Avi breathes out and stills her heart. At the right hand of Solomon sits Hiram – his banners black like the tabernacles of Kedar, emblazoned with an hart, the brilliant stag of Naphtali reflecting one-thousand flames' bright light.

Avi presses against the wall of the passage, in the dark. Her courage fails her in the brightness of the crowded hall.

That I might sit with my love, that his banner over me

was affection and protection. And still, with all his stunning radiance, the stag is yet lesser than the purple field and blazing golden sun of Solomon! And I hide frightened, a fornicator banished, an owl, a Lilith of the night.

Watching Hiram, she is frozen with indecision in the curtained corridor. He is surrounded all about. Beautiful women cling to him like vines, and he, a sweet fruiting tree, stands in a field of upright men.

She whispers, "Look how the outstanding of Israel love you. Because of the savor of your spirit, the honeybees swarm you. Your name... Hiram, is like ointment to an ailing ear, therefore the virgins love you. Yet, I love you more than all of these. Shallow pools are their emotions to mine. You have drawn up the waters of my love, and the feelings flowing now I much prefer to the slumbersome wine I have drunk to dumb my outcrying soul.

Looking now upon your bushy locks, black as corvid rooks, I am jealous. See how the little bees bustle, brushing your petal-soft ruddy white skin? These laced-winged laughing maidens sting my joy. I envy them your nectar. All the virgins love you, but I may not touch you; you, a blossomed lily in an orchard alive with thorns, and I stand without, barred by briars."

A voice ripples Avi's reflection; a mother, or a woman who loves her no less, Bathsheba, whose sloping breasts have caught the floods of Avishag's weeping eyes, whose sweet embrace has shuddered with her wilting cries.

"Who is it that stands concealed in the coal dark curtains? Who hides, a shadow, a wisp, deep in the flax-weaved linens?"

Her eyes can scarce perceive, but Bathsheba senses some past child she must have coddled. "Speak woman, that I might know you."

Avishag sobs. Hands hide her face. "Look not upon me. I am sun-kissed and dark."

Bathsheba's ears brightly hear, and she knows the voice, "Avishag?! Dark but comely." She gazes at the child she once guarded, now a lady grown. "You must not join the joyous guests, lest you receive unbearable reproof from the jubilant groom."

Silent tears slip the slopes of Avi's cheeks and trickle from her chin.

"My presence here deserves disdain! What disappointment fate has delivered me for destiny. Nearly ordained a queen, and now a vineyard girl, damned for the cursed quarrels of kingly brothers. Do not think low of me, Queen of Kings!"

"No! No! God has blighted you with beauty incomparable. All men that see you love you; yet, the love of men is banished from your unblessed life, and you are betrothed to sadness." Bathsheba cries for pity's sake and repentance. "Speak no more your speech of mourning. My heart breaks to hear you bawl. I'll speak to Solomon in the morning. To curse such a blessed creature is a sin. Such a crime cannot be forgiven. Let the king make recompense for unjust punishment. Be his wife, and he your husband."

Avi falls and groans the deeper. Her stomach clenched, fills with bitter feelings from words so sweetly spoken.

Bathsheba's bowels churn, roiled with regrets, compassion embosomed within her womb. "I must hail my son and wish him well. Follow now my servant girl, take refuge in my bed, and heal."

* * *

Hiram, all the men who hear you, love you; all the women who see you strive, that you might love them; but you are wilting, and those who would adore you, are as flies.

"Hiram," Solomon whispers, "what ails you?"

"I am sick with love, for she I love has forsaken me twice."

"Your sadness has made you a flower without nectar, a tree without shade, and all who come to you for pleasure have fluttered off, scathed and craving. Lift up your head. Rejoice this night before I wed. God has portioned all good things, and happy feelings are your worthy dues."

"Yes, my brother. Though with longing I would leap to mountain peaks, her love to me is as a tower that is locked and without stairs; she is always out of reach. And when to God I speak, and nightly beseech that he will give her me; it is as if I have come to feast, and he has given up my seat, and in my place a stranger sits to eat. No, let me think no longer on this woman. Stay my ague with drink, comfort me with sweets, and shortly I will greet your guests with a mirthful heart and glee."

"Perhaps, do not be gleeful now; drunken, muddled, and vexed. When sick with love, it is better to go to the house of mourning than to a feast. Sorrow is better medicine than laughter for a man scorned in such a manner. Go to my room and wallow while you wait. When I return to you tonight, melancholy will have washed your thoughts of bitterness, and I'll have words for you wiser than your desires."

Chapter 25:
A Wakeful Heart

In Solomon's chamber, the king speaks with Hiram, "My beautiful friend, why is your beloved greater than another beloved? You who are so crowded with women, a lily among the blooming saffron, who is this woman to any other, that for her sake your heart is cast down?"

"She is like wine that goes down sweetly, causing the lips of the sleeping to speak. No, how much better is her love than wine! The smell of her neck than all ointments. Her breath, like almonds. She is the North Wind, full of spice and pollen, seeding my fruits with pleasures."

"A northern breeze for my southern warden. That is pleasant. Your words are ointment. Yet, my friend, from all you say, this woman is a city walled and you have been ousted. How is it that you have known her? Mayhap, she is another man's beloved."

"I fear I tell too much. If she is married, she has sinned against her husband. I tell not all, but will say some. While I wandered through the many hamlets and hills, villages and vales of Israel, I found a pleasant place. I was happy there, so I went down into the arbors of almonds and apricots, to see the fruits of the valley and the flourishing flocks, and to smell the sweet budding pomegranates.

"I rested at a well, and before I was aware, was encircled about by young women and lovely girls. My lady was there, and my heart raced and thundered. I was filled with spirit, as is a man before war.

"I stayed there a while in her valley. I found her as gentle as the morning, fair as the moon, with wisdom as clear as the sun. Whenever I saw her, my chest was as the stamping feet of armies, driving me to her, come what may!"

Solomon searches his mind for a woman of such description, "Where is this valley? What is this woman's name who is so fine? Tell me, so that for your sake I might inquire whether she is wed, or perhaps may be bought with kine."

"If it is true that she is betrothed or wed to another, what impropriety, what a secret you beg of me, to ask the woman's name! I will not have her ruined, nor have her name defamed."

"Truly, truly, I will not ask again. If she is married you may not have her. If she is betrothed, it is likely no man would part with a woman so rare. Has she no equal? A serving girl? A sister?"

Hiram meets Solomon's gaze, "My dove, my unblemished is but one, an only daughter, the choice child of she that bore her."

* * *

In the queen's bed, Avishag sleeps, but her heart is awake. She dreams she wakes to the voice of her beloved.

"I am come into my garden, my dear sister, my spouse. I am lathered with myrrh. My skin steams with spice. I have eaten my honeycomb with the honey. I have drunk milk with wine. My friends and I, we are drunk! We have drank to abundance, and I am come to you in love, made miserable by your absence."

Avi answers him, "I must sleep. Yet my loins are moved with love, to open to you."

"Open to me Avishag, my dove, my undefiled beauty."

"I lie naked to sleep," she says. "I have removed my coat, a gift from Solomon, and I cannot put it on again."

"Please, my head is dappled with dew, my locks with drops of the night."

"I have washed my feet, I cannot defile them with dust."

Hiram's scent, a hand like the wind, reaches through the walls. Avi's belly churns with passion for her love. She rises from bed and goes to the door. Her hands seep with sap, and her fingers drip with myrrh upon the lock. She opens to Hiram, but he has withdrawn and is gone. Her soul fails. Only his scent remains, searching the room for her. She calls but hears no answer. She seeks him but sees him not.

She runs through the streets searching, and the city watchmen catch her.

"Have you seen my beloved," she asks, but receives no answer.

They smite and wound her, tear the veil from her tumbling hair.

She awakens, and is sick of love.

Chapter 26:
Shulamite Returned

A month has passed since the marriage, and Avishag has taken her place within the harem; groomed and combed, painted and adorned. The women envy her, and no man sees her. He who once ignored her, now might love her.

The king summons, and she sings. The women dance in metal speckled dresses, reeds in the wind of Avi's breath, and the voice of birds as the tinkling of brass. Her voice slides through Solomon and coils within his breast. He is captured. He marvels, as Moses at Jethro's daughters, like he who is lost in the wilderness and remembers the smell of water, or the scent of harvest that wafts the mellow fruit.

Solomon's desires draw him deeper into fascination for the forlorn woman. Many days he brings her gifts, and kisses her cheeks, and reads her poems — yet she is a secret garden of undisclosed pleasures. She is a gate locked. He grows restless. Lying at night in sleepless dreaming, his mind conjures love that in fleshed life is vacant.

He paces the many pillars of the court, measuring the span between them, pulling tight the cord that binds him clutching behind her. He seeks her out and finds her. His lion's heart cowers; so much his imagination has fortified her.

"I am tired. I am a running hound, winded from the chase. My pads are worn, and weary are my legs. When my mouth would bless you, you swiftly turn and my teeth bite wind. My tendons are tight to snapping. How long must I run before your fears are satisfied and you might be mine?"

She turns to him. "What little Solomon can know of wanting love. The greatest lover knows nothing of longing, uncertainty, the seeds of passion. Solomon, see now the sickness of love. Look close and see, not the drowning beauty of your obsession, but the teary cheeks of a downcast girl, your father's darling."

He falls between her knees. "Forgive me, Sister. How is it I have been so cold, when so warm a child needed care? How remiss, how foolish a fool am I. These many years, surely you have mourned unloved. I cup your face, precious living water in my hands. Forgive me. Like the spring, let our love be renewed. We will be married as is your due. You will be loved, as is your dessert. All will be well, and that in your life which has been rough will be hewn smooth."

Avi bathes his head with tears and answers him with sadness. "How long I awaited your pardon. How long I wished to be your partner. You left me, a plant to wither, no power to uproot, nor seek my want. You had power. You were a man, and I a soiled garment, rent and cast aside. Now another has found me. He has nourished me. He has cleansed and mended me. In him, I am fulfilled."

Solomon stands and understands. A righteous rage wells in him. "From the lion's jaws, from the grasping paws of the law, I hid you away! When stones raised to smash and smother you in bloody death, I gave you into the caring arms of brothers. Now, you revile me and rebuke my repentance. You revile me?! You who have sinned against me twice; first in secret meetings with my heartless brother; secondly, in some stranger's bed. You walk with death tied 'round your neck, a crushing millstone! How in my month of chasing I was a lolling dog; in my moment of remorse, a fool.

"I cannot rightly protect you. You have set yourself against the laws and traditions. Who should aid those who harm themselves? You were born to privilege, and yet have sunk to perdition."

Solomon calls his armed men. "Lock her away. She stands condemned."

Chapter 27:
Laughed to Scorn

Bathsheba, take pity on your ward. Let her not be scorned, cast down and stoned as an adulterer. Shield her from shame. Keep her from the wrath of Solomon.

Speaking to Solomon, she says, "Forgive her. It is not right that woman should be alone – Lonely, she will seek her counterpart."

Solomon speaks, "I may pardon once against Moses' Law and be called merciful. To forgive twice I would be a fool. Where first there was doubt, now there is confession. She has surely sinned, and must face justice' stoning hands. Behold, she has sinned against me. She has sinned against tradition."

"Forgive her, Solomon. Save her from the Law.

"As though the heavens have opened, your longing for her has overwhelmed you, as the longing does to all men. For do not the blessings of God bless all men. Does not the rain fall upon all fields; those of the worthy and unworthy alike? And do not all see her beauty and the blood rush from their hearts, and their passions burst forth like sprouting seed? Where she goes, life buds like spring's first grass.

"And yet, you plant no seed. Scorning the gifts of God, you refuse to love, and her fertile womb lies resting, fallow. Take her to be your wife. Enjoy the fruits of God's will. For none but a true king should possess such a queen. And no man shines brighter. No man is better. She will love you. She will love your wealth, your name, your fame. Whomever she has loved will be forgotten."

"Of all women, I would least expect such rhetoric from you; knowing love overcomes all propriety, and lust destroys husbands. With all my power, I cannot shift Avi's want. I cannot shade the sun. A man would be laughed to scorn, were he to try to buy love, whether by money, state or power."

"Once," says Bathsheba, "I was Avishag. I loved a king and had a servant. She loves a servant and has a king. I would not ask for compassion, except I know through mercy might come greater blessings. I would not seek Avi's pardon, if in me the greater sin did not rest. For the laws I transgressed, Israel has been doubly endued. A wiser man was never born of woman. A better king the law has never given."

"You speak short sighted speech. You have yet to stand before God in judgment. I speak candidly; that you may know your depravity is not condoned. God may yet smite you, even as poor Uriah was struck down, pierced through with an arrow. And Avi may strike me from my throne with as little remorse as you now show; seemingly filled with glee that your husband did bleed to death upon the battle's breast. Such craft must always meet its match in God. She shall surely die. So mote it be!"

Chapter 28:
In the Court of Women

Hiram, 'tis high noon. Hie now to the Holy of Holies. Address the Lord your God, as you daily do. For He is your friend, and your prayers have never importuned.

"Oh God, hear the words of my mouth. My arms are raised in adoration. Your temple nears its dedication, seven years from the setting of the corner stones for its foundation. The keystone of the royal arch is nearly finished. The capstone lies shrouded, polished, hidden, waiting to be raised. Thank you, oh Lord, for the part I have played."

A maiden waits within the Court of Women, waits for Hiram that she may inform him, and tell him of his love's hard fate.

"Hiram, hear the words of my mouth, attend the news I portend. I come on behalf of she you love. I bear news of Avishag."

"A month I waited, wished for word of her. Now I have hopes she will not return, but rather leave me to finish my work. Unhand me, woman."

"Please, Master Hiram! She shall surely die! Hiram, veer from your path of determination. Give ear to this woman whose tears holler to be heard."

"For what is she condemned? By whom has she been doomed?"

"She is accused an adulteress, a lecherous seductress. The king has spoken against her, demanding her death."

"Whom has she sinned against? Who is her husband?"

"She has sinned against Solomon, for she is his, betrothed from birth."

Hiram hides his face beneath his hands, hurries to shield his shame within the shade of the temple wall.

"With whom has she lain? Who would dare bed the concubine of our king?"

The woman answers, "You know. You are the man."

Hiram rips his shirt and grits his teeth. "Oh that the stones of the temple would bury me, for I cannot face my friend nor bear the consequence of my sins."

* * *

Hiram, speed down from the mountain, down into the city, down to Avi's cell. The guards will open to you; you who speak as a master, as with the voice of Solomon himself.

Avi reaches to hold him as he enters, but in anger he repels her.

"Why have you deceived me? Why have you tempted me to transgress? In my innocence, I laid with you. Though you knew that death could follow, you let me lie unknowing, blissful, naked in your sin-filled bed."

Avi cries. "Hiram, I have loved you as I shouldn't. I have led you into transgression, given you to taste what was forbidden. We drank of the vine and were drunk. Now, I pay the price of sin, which is death."

Hiram turns again to Avishag, his wrath no match for compassion. "Don't speak of death. Solomon will spare you, he loves me so."

"He will not, for he has once already spared me for love. Now, he burns with a most vehement flame of anger. His jealousy is cruel as the grave, hot as coals. It will not be subdued, and I shall die."

"What are coals to the many floods of sadness I will pour out to Solomon? What are whispering flames to my emotions, the rush of many waters? No more than a hiss, forgotten."

"Even so, if I shall die, set me as a seal upon your heart, that God might know we are joined."

"Love seals our souls, mine to yours, as the trowel seals stones, bound to never be broken. For love is strong as death."

Chapter 29:
I Am the Man

With a kiss and a grin the king greets his friend. "Hiram, what bears you to my chamber so late, when none listen and none awake?"

Hiram shakes. With words he trembles. "I have met a man in the temple. I have heard his confessions concerning a woman in the palace."

"Gossip, Hiram. You stand as though struck with fear. I have not seen you so consumed by cares."

"He told me of a king's daughter, loved by all who know her, now locked away; and her man, an adulterer."

"A shepherd girl, Hiram. A girl who guards a flock of goats. Hardly great. Hardly of note. She is the dust upon my sandals. Stop this thoughtless chatter, you who think of lofty thoughts. Let us rather speak of your accomplishments. You have brought glory to the land, beauty unrivaled and unforgettable."

"No," says Hiram, "I will speak of the woman. I know the import of her station. I know the implication of a king's concubine lying down with a man who is not king."

Solomon stands and turns from his friend. "You would draw me, like a bow, to my limits? Speak no more of this Hiram, or I shall surely snap, for you now pull tight the strings of my anger."

Yet, Hiram continues, " 'Great Beauty' the man said to me, 'Beauty unrivaled and unforgettable. I have loved a woman engaged. I have loved with a love that outlives death!' So spoke the man in the temple."

Solomon's rage now is sprung; a deadly man, his wrath unstrung. He breaks his chair and strikes his friend.

"Why do you provoke? Why do you break my heart? Who is this jackal? What coward hides whilst his love lies in shackles? Who laid with she who is my betrothed, and candidly shares his stories in the temple's court? He shall be stoned with heavy stones! Buried like mason's rubble beneath the crushing rocks! May he cry out for mercy and no brother hear him nor come to his aid!"

Hiram quakes. Silent droplets stream his face. "So mote it be, Friend. I am the man."

Solomon drops, despairing. "Hiram. Hiram. Hiram." The king covers his face. "Your love to me is better than that of women; my love to you, beyond the love of living. Have you deceived me, knowing that you betrayed?"

Hiram clings to his king's legs, his head on the thigh of his friend. "Never, my lord! I never would. I never will."

Solomon weaves his fingers through Hiram's hair and kisses his curly head. He holds him, rocking as a father with his dying infant. After many moments, he says, "The demands of justice are a heavy burden. In you, my throne is threatened. Go, leave me to mull, that I might weight the measures of mercy in your favor."

Hiram sticks to his place, "Will Avishag be safe?"

Solomon looks to his friend, "What righteous judgment may be passed? Is there any decree that I might make by which all might be saved? Avishag is an adulteress, which sin's punishment is death. And by the law, I must kill you also, my dearest friend. If I let you live, I will have raised you to the king's station, and so may fall David's kingdom; I, a cuckold to a craftsman. I have killed kin to be king. I have killed brothers for Avishag's sake. Now, you are at my throne, and the Law is at your throat. You ask if Avishag will be safe? Not one of us is safe. Now leave, and trust my rule to mete out righteousness."

Chapter 30:
A Listener at the Door

Solomon calls his wife, the Pharaoh's daughter.

"Come to me, Love, and see that none follow. Look out the door for priests, and out the eaves for listening ears. Let us whisper that none may hear, for a righteous man may die if loud lips proclaim these secrets."

"None are listening, my lord," she lies. Her maiden awaits her in the dark, a messenger to save Avishag from malice.

Solomon paces the cold stone floors. "A righteous man might sin against his friend, and yet not know his crime. And still justice clamors, and claims of spite might drive men to evil action. But what is friendship, what is brotherhood, if a brother should not forgive his friend? Even the vilest of deeds, though it rends one's heart, cannot steal love so strongly formed. So for love's sake, I must pardon when he whom I adore would repent. Yet punishment must be meted. But should I banish one of such worthy nature, to leave him to waste in the wilderness to die or become like some wily creature, to burn where only dust and lizards thrive... Then surely, greater would be my crime, for no better man was ever born of woman."

"You are perplexed, for the man you speak of is your brother, the grandmaster architect."

"He is the man. And my love for him is unbound, and his folly unplanned. So take him to Egypt. Take him to Pharaoh, that Egypt may be blessed, and this curse be reversed, and balance be brought by the land of your birth."

"I will go, and I will do as you command. My father will hire your masterful man, and he whom you love will be saved. But what of my love? What of the lovely Avishag? It is good to forgive one's friend, but even the hypocrites do this. Who is the better king than God? And does not God cause the rain to fall upon those he loves, as well as those he hates? Man may never satisfy justice, so rather let us mercy sate."

"To sin unknowing may be called innocence. We are all fools, and vanity may cloud our reason, but to sin the same sin twice, this can only be a crime. Once when Avishag was young, I saved her from the crushing stones, but now she is grown, a woman, and a treacherous one. She has lured a godly man down into bed, a bed whose fruits of love bore seeds of death, and yet she hid the truth, that she has been betrothed since youth. She should surely die."

The king speaks on, but the woman hidden in the dark listens no more. She runs to the camp of the Shulemites. She runs to warn the Jubaalim of Avishag's plight.

Chapter 31: Judgment

Hiram, Solomon has made a way for you. He has pulled you from the pit, and set you on the path to love. When the gaping mouths of dungeon and tomb waited, open to consume, Solomon has saved you. Praises to the wise king, wise beyond his youth.

Hiram kneels before his king.

"You must leave Jerusalem, Hiram, even Israel. The craft are filled with wrath. Like unto the brothers of Joseph, the sons of Jacob, they are jealous, breathing hatred with cries for justice. You are not safe, nor am I secure if you shelter here. You shall dwell in Egypt the remainder of your days, a guest among his greatest architects. You will be banished, but free in Egypt."

"My lord, you are mighty as you are merciful, yet, what is mercy to me if Avishag should not be free."

"These many nights I have pondered, my pillows I have watered, and I have judged; what God has joined, I will not sunder. Avishag has left for Egypt. I release her bonds to me, that she may be bound in fullness with you. So be it."

Hiram laughs and leaps with joy. He embraces his lord, and they rejoice together.

Solomon directs Hiram further, "Make haste, Hiram. You must hie away. There are hissings concerning you and I. The angry men of Shulem have gathered with the brothers of Avishag, the Jubaalim, believing you have done them wrong."

"What's this you say? The rough men of Tyre? My hard hands of justice are Avishag's brothers?"

"The same, as you say. All the Shulemites I have sent away with their pay, that no mobs may form. Their anger is as furious as their strength is famous. Should you meet them in the street, flee. And may your feet have wings.

"That you must cease as builder of the temple, I bemoan. Your absence will eternally be mourned. No other man can craft a home for the Lord so well as you, for the Lord resides in your heart, and all your works of art are a sacred reflection of his spirit. Stay a single Sabbath more with me, to show your master masons the intricacies you have planned. Choose wisely your replacement, and the temple shall stand atop the hills, a monument to the strength of God."

"Thank you, my lord. Though I grieve my unfinished work, I rejoice in my future, and bless your name forever."

"It is nothing for a man to bestow mercy on a friend. All men would do this. Now, prepare. You have a rough and rugged road before you."

* * *

At high-noon Hiram kneels alone in the Holy of Holies, there are none to hear him pray. He hails his God and delights in his mercies. With tears he waters the dust that veils the sacred silence in white.

Brethren in the darkened doors, hear; Hiram walks upon the temple's floors, his steps lively upon the stones. Hiram leaves his hallowed room, rejoicing, crossing the courtyard laughing out his lordly praise. Leave him now, you brothers of the song, you Jubaalim. Feed not your fury with righteous blood. You hate-filled men, hidden in the dark, remember you your inception to the craft, when all was ignorance and black, and you longed for sight, the light you lacked. And you, like Hiram, fatherless, knew not what was before you, and Hiram received you in loving hands. Leave now the city. Sleep now with your brethren among the tents. Leave off this mission of vengeance. Do right, be square. Leave poor Hiram. Harm him not at his place of prayer, lest he be a martyr, and you all, murderers.

Leaping, laughing, singing out his praise, Hiram walks toward the southern gate, where waits Jubela with hands clenched like claws. He grabs his master, yanks his clothes.

"Long have I awaited this moment, Grand Master Hiram. Fortuitously, I find you alone."

"You break the law Jubela, having brought with you an instrument of metal into the temple. What violence is in your thoughts?"

"Many call you great, Hiram. Never would I have denied the veracity of their claims. Now, I recoil to hear your praise. My family, my people are despoiled. Plotting your elevation, many heads you have laid beneath your feet, striking with your heels the servants, humble and sorely used. Our strong men have been made meek. Our mourning women you have shamed."

Hiram shirks the man's rough and grasping hand. "What harm have I done to you? To what do you allude?"

"To the men of Salem who have served devotedly, and my family, my dearest Avishag, who surely now lies dead beneath a pile of stones."

Hiram your face has fallen. Fly now, Hiram. May your feet have wings!

Jubela swings his brazen gauge and gashes his master's throat.

Hiram flees, wishing that some loyal workman might hear him wailing.

"HELP! BROTHERS, HELP!"

Is there no help for poor Master Hiram?

Now comes aid to Jubela; his brother Jubelo at the West gate. Hiram grabs hold of him.

"Jubelo! Jubelo! Let there be love in your heart. Remember you our friendly discourse these many years."

Jubelo wrestles Hiram, and Jubela grabs hold his master from behind.

"Why, brothers? Hear from me the truth! Be men, not brutes. Lend an ear of mercy to me, your friend from youth. I have only loved and loyally treated your sister, and your people I never abused. All will be set right. Let me be, that you may sleep free tonight. Go back to your wives. Go to your children, that they be not also widows' sons."

"Lie no more! Feign no kindness. Without care you have swived our sister, and without compassion Solomon has condemned her to death. Years have we served Solomon and bided your commands as fellows. Working endless hours, these many years we have shaped stones to your, our master's plans. Years have you promised us the secrets of the master masons. Yet, we and all Shulemites have at the peak of our ascension been cut off, out-cast, refused to the last man. See, beyond the walls of Jerusalem is a host of tents, men promised master's wages, master's knowledge, that they may leave when the work is accomplished, and find worthy hire in foreign lands. We know you will flee to Egypt. But what of us? What of our sister, whom you reject as a garment soiled and rent."

Hiram pleads, "Your sister is free! You shall be given all you deserve, as agreed. Act worthily and surely in due time you will be risen to the ranks of those who have gone before."

"Enough! Our servant has heard Solomon. He has said our sister deserves no mercy! We have been paid and our wages were wanting. Banished men will find no place in the world of kings! Now you will suffer what is just!"

Hiram grips and throws. Jubela crumples, smacked against the stones, but Jubelo hacks at Hiram's chest, cutting wide his breast with a mason's square made of brass.

"GOD! OH MY GOD!" Hiram cries. Blood spatters the chalky floors, mists the dust-fogged air that clouds his choking screams. He batters his assailants, overcomes their grasping hands. Onward he speeds, fleeing to the eastern gate.

Is there no help for the widow's son?

Jubelum awaits him there, a heavy hammer in his hand. He grabs the dying man, thrusts him to the ground with earnest strength. "You have escaped Jubela. You have escaped Jubelo. You will not escape me. For, what I purpose, that I perform. I hold in my hand an instrument of death. Repent, that we might be justified."

Hiram wilts, frothy mouthed and soaking crimson red

with life from every pore. "I will not repent the blessings which God has given me... Rather, repent you. Have you no remorse for a widow's son?"

"God has deserted Moriah. We all go fatherless. Repent, and blood will atone for you the wrongs afflicted upon the people of Salem!"

Hiram says, "I cannot."

"Then die!"

Jubelum strikes Hiram's brow with a mighty blow, loud as splitting stone. The brothers' faces splash with blood. The great man lays in quivering death that shakes the ground. Hiram's light bursts forth. He is no more.

How is it none have heard him cry? How is it none have come to aid the beautiful man of Naphtali? Is there no mercy in the hearts of men? Now he lies dead, his joy never to be heard again, his brilliance never to walk the polished temple floors.

See how the brothers loom over the corpse of their smitten master. They quake, energized by their evil act.

"Look now upon the work of our hands. Oh! How the mighty are fallen. Our master we worshipped, so full of love, was but a vile man, now laid low, his last breath a gust upon the temple floor.

"With what grandiosity he strutted through our ranks, with what grasping hands he took what was not his, and withheld that which is ours. And now his head lies low, black hair in the dust of the temple floor."

Jubelum is quick to act. He grabs Hiram's arms and drags him to the rubble. The brothers bury him deep in stones and dust. With their masons aprons they mop the blood from the floor of the courtyard. The crimson stained skins will never wash clean, the red blood of Hiram will remain, a testament to their misthought deed.

"Let us scatter, lest one of us is caught, they will not find the others. At low twelve, we will meet again to take his body from the city in the middle of the night. And we will disappear from Israel."

The three are agreed and hide themselves within the city, awaiting darkness.

* * *

The brothers reunite at low twelve in the courtyard of the temple. They bundle Hiram up and haul him away. Like a king, they place his body upon an ass. They flee for the valleys of Sharon, their home.

Chapter 32:
The Empty Trestle Board

Solomon, awake! Rejoicing and loud laughter! A terrific roar rises from the temple! The men wander home.

"Bless Hiram, wherever he may be!" the craftsmen say. "The trestleboard is wiped clean. The masters have no designs for we fellows. Bless Hiram, wherever he may be!"

There is confusion, a raucous shuffling not fit for hallowed ground. Go down to the temple, see to it there is order; harmony being the strength and foundation of every great endeavor, most of all the building of the House of the Lord.

Solomon slams the gavel down. "Why are you idle? What is this chatter and prattle? Where is your warden? Where is Hiram?"

All answer, "None have seen our master since high twelve yester-noon."

"High noon?! Call roll. Call all men back from home. Call a strict search of the temple grounds. Hiram must be found!"

Solomon, Wise and Worshipful King, the callers have called and all have answered, none amiss. When beckoned, all returned.

Solomon deliberates upon the dutiful nature of his mislaid friend. *Hiram, my beloved companion, surely some harm has befallen you. My heart shrinks to think what evil has found you.*

Solomon speaks to Hiram's second, "Go down to the

camp of the Shulemites. Call them all to account. See if any have seen Hiram. When all have been questioned, return and report."

* * *

Solomon sits alone. Report returns from the Shulemite encampment. Runners kneel before the throne.

"Lord Solomon, there are three missing, who when summoned did not answer; rough ones, Jubela, Jubelo, and Jubelum, known as the Tyrian Brothers, though they be from Shulem."

Solomon, still as a stone, rises not from his chair. "My dread deepens and my soul despairs to envision the malfortune of my brother, Hiram. It is as I feared, that these three fellows should not be found."

A knock is heard at the door, a messenger enters the room, yet, there cannot be fine words nor kind fortune, for Hiram no longer lives, but abides a hidden crypt. All words are a chorus of wretched gloom to Solomon, whose bosom brother is gone, likely consumed by the worms of an earthen tomb.

"King Solomon, an emissary of twelve fellowcraft have come from the Shulemite camp and ask admittance to enter the city, that they might have audience of the king."

"Let them enter and bring them to me," answers the king.

The twelve fellowcraft stand before Solomon. They wither at his gaze, grass shriveled in the sun's beaming rays.

"What word of Hiram do you have? And if none of

Hiram, what of these Brothers of Tyre?"

The foremost speaks, "We come to you, Lord, with our gloves and aprons supple, powdered white with stone, that you may see we are unstained and clean from any blood. Yet, we fear we have conspired to murder, and seek redemption for our collusion."

Solomon stands with his sword in hand and nearly swings to swipe the head from the shoulders of the man. He refrains. "In what way have you schemed against Hiram?"

The begging man begins, "We fifteen were agreed and rash with anger; for having served as stone cutters these several years, we were forced to leave our labors. Having thus been uninvolved without righteous cause, we grew in ire, knowing we had been robbed of a master's rights to travel and seek worthy hire wheresoever we would desire. Our wages were less than pledged, and we placed this evil on Hiram's head. Together we planned to capture our master and force his cooperation in raising us to the level of master masons. Reflecting on our master's pleasant person, we twelve disavowed this plot. Today, having heard that our Lord Hiram was missing, we shook with guilt, and frought with fear shivered with fright. We met together, and all proved our innocence, but three did not come to absolve their part. We fear they have murdered Hiram. Please understand, we here are supplicants, that our part in this crime was not innocence, and yet we bow before you with pure white hands. We have come, that this crime might be known, and that there may be justice for a worthy man."

Solomon says, "It is as I thought. My worries were warranted. Avishag's brothers have repaid me evil for good, to the bereavement of my soul. Go now, organize into four groups of three, one for each, the east, the west, the south and north. Find Hiram and his murderers, or all of you shall atone in blood for Hiram's death!"

Chapter 33:
Departure Denied

The Plains of Sharon, so sacred and secluded, Avishag's refuge, so untouched by royal violence, the sanctuary of love and safe childhood, is now the hidden site of her lover's morbid bed. Beneath the ground of the shepherds' haunt now lies Lord Hiram.

So speaks Avishag's brother, Jubelum, "Here in the hilly country of our home, we end this gruesome journey. Here beneath these cliffs of stone we bury Hiram, the so-called master of every craftsman.

"Let his grave be unmarked. Let the grasses seed this place of death, and may this place be forgotten by all but us. And may we be reminded, should we ever return, that none are loyal, none are firm, but brothers in blood are the only men that we can trust; for there is no love in the hearts of men, only words of fealty feigned."

There they leave a bare patch of soil where once was the most enlightened mind in all the lands surrounding the Lord's fair Jerusalem. A pile of dirt, cast vulgarly without rite, now cloaks the most brilliant of Israel's lights.

* * *

The brothers have sped to the port at Joppa, seeking a ship that will carry them oversea.

Say the brothers to each other,

"We have sought passage from these many captains,

and none will permit us aboard without a master's pass. Here we are land ridden, so long as we are only fellowcrafts."

"Then let us stay hidden until night and steal for ourselves a raft."

"We are men of rock not of brine. These vast waters are rarely kind. Who will pilot us when the sea is disturbed, and disaster threatens to drag us down to death?"

"We as yet cannot cross the sea. In a small craft we'd be caught up, and none of us understand the sailors' skills. We are land bound. But let's not stay here. I fear those that search for Hiram will quickly catch our trail, and should they capture us, they will kill us.

"Let us stay in Joppa for one night, and if any will let us stow in their hold, we will cast away with them at dawn. But if none will show kindness, we will return inland, and say we are traveling shepherds, nomads with no home."

"Let us ask these last few ships. One looks quite large and must be going far. If we could but cross to the other coast, we could conceal ourselves in a country where we'd be free. Mayhap, we will not have work with stone, but everywhere there are sheep to shepherd and goats to goad."

Look, you brothers! Look down the docks to the last ship. There, laughing, are maidens, fair as queens every one, and among them, Avishag. She like a princess billows with silks and Egyptians' soft linens, and she smiles like a woman swooning with her love's sweet words.

"See there on that ship? There stands our sister with the resplendent wife of Solomon, the Pharaoh's daughter. Here she is, ready to set out to sea, when we all thought surely she was dead, never again to be seen. Yet she is healthy, she is weal, and joyful.

"And now my bowels churn to think of what we have done to our beloved friend, Hiram.

"Like a stone thrown, hatred gave our anger wings, but now my soul sinks. My spirit descends the flood of the blood dark sea of shame. In the deep black of guilt, not a glimmer of hope can be seen, and my groans are drowned in the salts of sadness: for the Lord will surely not heed such an one who has done so evil a deed.

"Let the waves cover me, that none may hear, none may see, none may know what has come of the fool who was Jubelo."

"Look away and hide! From her happy station she has seen us."

Your brothers have turned their downcast faces, but you look on, Jubelum. As though through a fog, she doesn't know you. Her gaze is glazed as if she sees nothing, but looks on to a future thought.

"Forgive me, Sister. I knew not that you were loved."

Chapter 34: Regret

The brother's have returned to Sharon, their hearts guilt-burdened. So say they at the grave of their murdered friend,

"Here we stand again atop the hills of our home, to make sacred the grave in which is laid Hiram Abif.

"Here in anger resolved we stood before with curses in our mouths, but now we gaze to Heaven in hopes that God will listen and hear our heartrending cries for repentance. In our ignorance we have killed a man most loving and loved. In our passion we have laid low Hiram, the son of a gentle widow – and have left Hiram also childless. The lone son of his father, he is a line ended.

"We left his grave unmarked, that none would know where he lay, but have returned to make right the site of so great a man's final place. We do not know the rites as performed by holy priests, but rather pray for our master's eternal peace in the bosom of his mighty God. And we place at the head of our friend, a simple sprig, the acacia, the burning bush of wisdom, the marker and reminder of the Master Mason's glorious mind, forever lost to murder by fools and fiends.

"We mark this holy spot, that he will not be forgotten, but all passing will know a man lies here, an one to be thought well of."

* * *

Solomon's tiler announces the return of the twelve Shulemite fellowcraft.

"The twelve conspirators have reconvened here, Lord Solomon, and wish an audience with you."

The twelve enter and report.

"Lord Solomon, we have searched the several directions and found that three men caused suspicion at Joppa, asking the captains for passage to foreign lands. Those three, it was said, were seen walking inland."

Solomon commands that they follow him to the valley the ruffians call home, the plains of Sharon.

* * *

Solomon and his men stand together with the twelve at Avishag's house at the base of the hills, sitting, of all the houses, closest to the well.

Solomon commands them, "Go forth. Overturn every stone. Uproot every bush, that these brigands may be brought to justice. If you find them, subdue them, and if need be, pay with your lives for your part in the conspiracy. If they flee, give chase. Truly, you have no choice. It is their lives or yours. Either you or they will die for the murder of Hiram. Absolve yourselves by might or swiftness of feet. By whatever means, bring those men to me."

* * *

Three fellowcraft and their guards stand together atop the hill on which Hiram is laid.

"Let us rest here, from which place we can overlook all the valley. If any of the others should flush those brothers, like beaters a fox, we will see them from this height, like hawks look down from the lofty all-seeing sky."

Says another to himself, "I will find myself a place to rest. Perhaps on this bare patch, I will lay me down to nap."

And grabbing hold of a small shrub to set himself down, he uproots it stem and all.

"Curious, that a plant of such deep tap should so easily snap!"

"Curious more, that all is grassy but this ground where you had sat to lay down. Should we say we have found a grave?"

"No! Wait! Listen! Who sings?"

"'Tis the Brothers Jubaalim."

"What strains of sorrow! What sadness now harrows my soul, and strains my heart to outpour."

Listen, Fellows, listen to Jubelum and Jubelo. Hear Hiram's lament. Two men who were the great master's friends, now mourn their grievous sin. Those whose trust should have been as sure as stone, their bonds as strong as cement, now shed tearful song for he whom they have slain.

All who hear the brothers sing, weep. And the fellows feel the part they played in laying their master to an early grave. They all shake with quiet sobbing to hear the song of the Jubaalim.

"Oh that we could show mercy!"

"Truly, I too am moved. My spirit fails to hate after

the words I have heard. I am cheerless as the winter, to kill these men. Those were not the songs of the cold of heart. Can the guilty beget such grief?"

Go now, brethren. The slaying of Hiram cannot be unanswered, his blood undrained, nor his silver cord restringed. He lies dead beneath your feet, where once bounty blossomed by his every step. He lies dead where once he laughed, and leapt, and sped to hold his beloved.

Those whose lament is pure, and heartfelt weep, still have murdered a man so sweet, that there is no word, there is no grief that will bring their earthly minds reprieve for the sin of slaying one so perfect as Hiram Abif.

"There, sitting sleeps Jubela at the mouth of the cliff's crack."

Speed now men, though they be your kin, and princes of your land, lay bronze to them. Let your hearts be calm for the deed you are commanded to perform. Capture or kill their watchman, for he is twice a traitor now; first to his master, and now as a tiler to his brothers.

Quietly, swiftly they ascend the slope. With swords in hand, they rush the crag. Before the youngest brother wakes, they hack off his head, and his body drapes his seat, a bloody slab.

They've caught them now, like foxes gone to ground. They shall not escape the hunters' clubs, nor the hounds' tearing teeth. With flashing swords and gnashing mouths they subdue the brothers in their catching hands, and bring them bound down the mound to Solomon who waits near the house at the base of the mount.

Solomon sits before them. "When we were boys, we all

clasped arms and embraced in love. We all swore with sacred signs of brotherhood to protect our own and uphold those who fall. But you three jealous brothers, unrighteous judges, full of rotten courage sought poor Hiram out.

"My heart withers, and my liver shrivels to know men so close were deceivers. Truly, men are never true. God made only the stars constant and the constellations sure."

Jubelum answers, "None of us are of the stars, Lord, but all are of the mould. When we were trapped in that canyon like tods to earth, it brought to mind my father's words, 'Catch you the little foxes; the little foxes that spoil the grapes and worry the lambs.

"Remember, Jubelo, in our youth, when the men told us, 'Catch us the little foxes, the foxes that spoil the grapes and rob the vines?'

"We'd catch them, and Avishag would beseech us to spare them. She loved foxes, so we couldn't bear to harm them, but let them go. And she'd give them ewe's milk, though they'd grow to spoil the grapes and rob the vines.

But when we grew into men, our compassion waned, and when they were weaned, we'd club them. Their beauty marred. Their sleek fur matted. Their tails, each, a brush of blood. And Avi could smell their sweet odor on our hands.

"What joy fled her then. What joy we robbed from her. What happiness we spoiled.

"The smell of kits, so is Hiram's blood on our kid-skin gloves."

And Jubelo weeping speaks, "We were born the sons of peace, the heirs to Salem, and became the brothers of the song, the men of joy, Jubela, Jubelo, and Jubelum. But now my voice cracks to sing, for what sorrow we have brought with all our pacts that came to nought when anger drove us beyond the grasp of reason and of thought.

"There, on the mount, our brother's head is severed from his neck, and he lies a corpse above our friend... Forgive me... I choke to speak, and swallow many tears... It were better we'd never been born, for our lives now cannot be borne. Forgive us. And may the Lord look upon us soon with pity and no shame."

"Forgive me..." says Solomon. "So too are my hands stained."

And he kisses each their head, and kills them.

"The foxes of the plains, so were they."

Chapter 35:
Wake not Love

Standing at the ship's prow, Avishag looks out and down upon the water. She crosses the sea to await her love in the land of the lily-laden Nile. She laughs with joy to know that Hiram follows to join her in Egypt.

She says to Pharaoh's daughter, "How many times I have heard the refrain, 'Do not wake love.' But there is no choice. There is no time one may choose to let it sleep, or stir it up.

"It is in the Lord's hands.

"Each of us struggle, and some die to love or to resist that urge that cleaves us together. But the currents that pull apart and collide cannot be swum against.

"'Do not wake love.' 'Do not love.' Or 'Love now, love now him, and no other!' These are false commands, impossible demands! For the Lord gives, and the Lord takes. What he joins we cannot break, and what he cracks we cannot joist.

"So rather, do not seek to wake. Do not seek to let sleep that love which will choose of itself to beat with life so strong it cannot rest. But rather find peace, and flow, as the fragile bubble upon the frothy waves. For you have no power to say, 'I will now rise, or now descend.' The wave has chosen for us all, and we are naught but the foam, full of terror in the sinkings, and overcome with ecstasy upon the surge – and surely, every one will burst and be no more, as surely as we all shall die, without choice, and without will nor consent.

"We do not know when love will wake and cling to us, and when it does, neither do we have the will to subdue what is so potent. And when that love flees from us, because what wakes in our heart sleeps in another's, we have not the forces to contain it.

"So, you daughters of Jerusalem, be fruitful and free! And flow, as the foam upon the sea. Surge and plunge, and may His will be done!"

The End

Thank you for reading AVISHAG. If you enjoyed this book, please leave a review on Amazon, Goodreads, or wherever you purchase books. Leaving a review helps support the author's work, and gets the word out to other readers.

Made in the USA
Middletown, DE
13 September 2023